Mug Shot

Patricia Fisher Mystery

Adventures

Book 7

Steve Higgs

Dedication

This book is dedicated to Simonai Carbajal, Kate Sturgeon, and Susan K Mest, three readers who were able to correctly identify the person staying in cabin 34782. That person's identity was left as a big cliff-hanger at the end of *Frozen Vengeance*.

Great detective work on their part, but if you haven't read *Mug Shot* and want to know who it was, you'll have to keep reading – this is a no spoiler zone.

Table of Contents

A Shot in the Dark

My stomach growled dangerously when I spied the tray of canapes coming my way. Verity spotted it too and murmured, 'Thank goodness. I was beginning to feel faint.' Verity wasn't about to starve to death though; she carried a few extra pounds on her hips, which on a frame not much taller than five feet made her a little dumpy.

The canapes appeared to be a tray of blinis with a dab of avocado beneath a delicate pink prawn which had a curl of cucumber looped around it. They looked so immaculate, perfect, and exact that the chef preparing them must have taken minutes to create each one. They were arranged on a rectangular tray like the Horse Guards Regiment on parade. I would have been happy with a mini sausage on a stick with a knob of cheese.

The steward holding the tray was still coming our way, but then Verity and I had strategically positioned ourselves close to where they exited the kitchen but without getting so close that we appeared to be hanging around outside the door.

My name is Patricia Rose Fisher. I'm a soon-to-be divorced, childless woman in her early fifties with an unresolved relationship dilemma, a nose for trouble, and a benefactor who just happens to be the third richest man on the planet. How the last bit came about is an interesting story for another time, but a few months ago I was cleaning houses for chump change and now I have my own butler and I am cruising the globe on the world's finest luxury ship while staying in its biggest suite. I have blonde hair shot through with silver above an average figure and average looks. These are not things I spend much time thinking about.

Back home in England, I have a seventy-three room mansion to live in, courtesy of the same benefactor, and my own detective agency which was currently on hold because I was on the run (sort of) from a madwoman who calls herself the Godmother. She is at the top of an international organised crime syndicate, or something like that. She lives in a shadow world that no one seems able to penetrate, so the police asked me to make myself scarce while they did their best to stop her from killing me and everyone I know.

Today, the Aurelia is in Reykjavik, Iceland, undergoing repairs to its hull and several other systems that were damaged during a spree of sabotage events. According to the captain, an unfairly handsome man with whom my relationship dilemma exists, we would be good to leave in three days' time. The original stop off in Iceland had been set for two days, but we had been here for three already and arrived a day late. The passengers had all been suitably compensated with onboard spending money and with the lure of additional discounts on future bookings. I was unbothered about the delay and had greatly enjoyed having a longer stop ashore where I got to explore a place I had never been and might never return to.

Tonight, I was back on board with a new friend, a woman I met less than a week ago and who saved my life just a short while after when she killed a man with a spearfishing gun. Together, we were attending a party thrown by internet billionaire Howard Berkowitz and his wife Shandy. It was a last-minute thing, the invitation that is, not the party. I met Shandy two days ago when I was coming back from a jog around the deck with my pair of miniature dachshunds. She was staying in the suite next door, her husband having more than enough money to afford to rent it. She gushed at my dogs, and we hit it off.

Like me, Shandy came from a working-class background, that her father was a carpenter was one of the first things she revealed, and she expected to spend her life in blue-collar jobs trying to make ends meet. She met and married Howard, who was backpacking around the world at the time, twenty-five years ago and had their reception in the room above a pub in her small hometown in New Zealand. Five years ago, Howard came up with a website idea called walkmydog.com. It paired people with dogs and jobs with older, retired people who either couldn't afford to get a dog or didn't feel they had enough years left to justify getting one. It went global in less than a year and now he is measured among the richest people on the planet.

Shandy, a thinnish woman with naturally curly, bordering on unruly, hair, dark brown eyes, and a dominant nose that many others might have taken to a plastic surgeon to get fixed, pointed out that a billion isn't that much anymore, but she laughed while doing it in an embarrassed way.

Today was their twenty-five-year anniversary and they had thrown a party for two hundred guests in the main ballroom on the top deck of the Aurelia. I chose Verity as my plus one instead of Barbie because my perfect, size-zero, blonde friend had gone back to her job in the upper deck gymnasium. Verity and I were very similar in age; she was a year older, but we had a lot in common, and it felt like she was someone I might be able to stay in contact with when I got home. Most of the people I met on board I would never see again.

The tray of canapes drifted closer, but just as I was about to catch the steward's eye and lift my hand to grab one, or maybe ten, of the blinis, Shandy swooped.

'No, no, no,' she tutted. 'Where is the Master of Ceremonies? The blinis are not due yet. What is wrong with him? The hot canapes should be served first, followed by the watermelon sorbet. Goodness, please take this back.'

She wasn't rude to the man, but her behaviour surprised me, nevertheless. I didn't know her very well, and perhaps I had misjudged the kind of woman she was. Now that I was looking at her, I could see something else in her eyes; it looked like worry.

The steward, looking embarrassed, scuttled back to the kitchen while my stomach roared its disappointment. When Shandy turned my way, I must have still been looking disappointed because Verity jabbed my ribs with an elbow.

'Hello, Patricia,' Shandy smiled. 'I'm so glad you were able to come.' She closed the distance to us, reaching out to shake Verity's hand. 'Hello, I'm Shandy Berkowitz.'

'Verity Tuppence,' Verity replied. 'Congratulations on your anniversary and thank you for letting me share it with you.' Verity had leapt at the chance to come to what she referred to as a 'high roller' party. She left her husband, Walter, in their cabin where he would happily entertain himself, she assured me. They had been married for close to thirty years and I wouldn't say the relationship had gone sour, but I had spent a little time with them and they rarely spoke to each other and I had never seen them touch except for one occasion when they held hands briefly. Verity did all the talking and I secretly believed Walter was glad for a few hours' peace.

I guess Shandy felt she needed to explain her behaviour for, without prompting, she asked, 'Was I awful to that poor steward?'

Verity started making noises, trying to make Shandy feel better by playing it down. I opted for the truth. 'A little, Shandy, yes. Is everything okay?'

Shandy cast her eyes down and then back up a moment later, a tiny tear in the corner of her left eye which she swiped at instantly, laughing at herself while looking miserable. 'Oh, goodness. What must you think of me? It's my anniversary. I am married to a billionaire. Supposeably these things ought to be enough to make a person happy.'

Verity and I moved closer, shielding Shandy from other eyes that might notice her emotional state. 'Whatever is the matter, love?' Verity wanted to know. 'Is it Howard? Does he beat you?'

I don't know where Verity got that idea from, but it was met with an aghast look from Shandy. 'No. Howard would never hurt me. It's nothing really,' she attempted to dodge explaining.

'It clearly isn't,' my argument stopped her from escaping without offering us something more.

She blew out a hard breath and let her shoulders slump as she brought her emotions back into check. 'I have a stalker,' she revealed. 'Or we have a stalker to be more accurate.' Now the cat was out of the bag, she accepted that she needed to tell us more. 'There have been some anonymous emails. Even when we block them, they just come through from a different source. Then we got a proper letter, but it was typed and not handwritten. That came this morning and it wished us good luck on our anniversary.'

'That doesn't sound threatening,' said Verity, sounding confused.

Shandy looked at her. 'It ended by telling us we deserved everything we have coming.'

I felt a chill roll down my back and could only imagine what it might be like to believe there was someone after you but you had no idea who they were so they could be anyone, including the person standing next to you. Oh, wait a second. I know exactly what that is like because that's the deal I have with the Godmother.

I didn't get to ask Shandy anything further about it because another woman approached us. She looked like a younger, prettier version of Shandy. Her hair and features were too similar for the two women to not be related, but the younger woman's features were softer, or proportioned just a little better, and the difference was surprising.

'There you are,' she said as she placed a hand on Shandy's arm. 'Howard wanted to let you know he is going to make a speech in a couple of minutes.'

Shandy turned her head to acknowledge the new person joining us. 'Ladies this is my little sister, Bubbles.'

'Bubbles?' Verity and I both echoed together.

Bubbles snorted a wry laugh. It was clear her name was an old joke. 'That's what dad used to call me. No one else has for thirty years except my old sister.' She hit the 'old' part of her sentence hard to contrast it wickedly with Shandy calling her little. 'Hi, I'm Grace.' She had her phone in her right hand, a bright red, sparkly case on it I noticed when she switched it to her left hand so she could offer the right to shake.

Verity and I shook hands with Grace, but she was there to steal the hostess away and we let her go without a fight. There were lots of people to mingle with and meet; I liked the parties on board the Aurelia, but I really did need something to eat. When the kitchen door opened again a moment later, I threw politeness and decorum out of the window and barrelled over to block the steward's path.

Shovelling tiny crostinoes into my mouth as delicately as one can, the polite sound of a spoon on the side of a glass brought my attention around to a space at the edge of the room. Howard was about to say some things. Howard stood over six feet tall, with sandy coloured hair that was beginning to thin. He was handsome, but not in an athletic way. Rather, his blue eyes and easy smile made him easy to look at.

People drifted closer, forming a loose circle around where he stood. 'Thank you, all, so much for coming this evening.' He was making standard speech statements and, no doubt, would shortly say many kind things about his wife. Half listening to what he was saying, I looked about for Shandy but couldn't see her. There were a lot of people, so she had to be hidden by the press of them around her husband.

I had one little crostino left, which I popped into my mouth. It was barely big enough to bother chewing, but I washed it down with what was left in my champagne glass and settled in to listen to what Howard had to say. He wore a big smile, that was fuelled, a little, by alcohol if his rosy cheeks were anything to go by. He was standing on the stage at the front of the room, a platform elevated by about a foot over the rest of the deck and had command of his audience.

'I think it's time I share with you all, a short anecdote from our wedding night,' he suggested cheekily, a twinkle in his eyes as his smile broadened yet further.

I expected to hear a groan from Shandy or maybe even a shout of protest that he shouldn't dare, but I was not expecting the lights to go out.

The ballroom was plunged into sudden and very complete darkness. There were several screams, and cries of surprise from both men and women, but almost everyone screamed in shock when the first shot was fired.

Instinctively I ducked, grabbing Verity's arm to pull her with me to the deck. The room lit for a nano second when the gun fired, the effect like lightning, only more fleeting. A second shot followed the first, the sound deafening, but cringing as I waited for yet more shots to be fired, what I heard instead, amid the terrified cries of alarm, was a keening noise of anguish and the sound of someone struggling for breath.

Verity grabbed my hand where it held her hand, transferring my hand into hers where she gripped it tightly. 'Patricia what do we do?' she wailed.

The lights came back on with the same suddenness with which they were extinguished. They had been off for no more than ten seconds, but it was long enough for the dimmed, party-atmosphere light level to now seem harsh. I blinked against it, checked around, and clambered back to my feet because there was no sign of anyone with a gun.

My nice dress was covered in dust and stuff from the floor where I had got onto my belly, but I didn't care about that. I wanted to know who fired the shots and whether the threat had been eliminated. But also, who was hurt?

Catching movement from the corner of my right eye, I spotted the white uniforms of ship's security running toward the stage. There had been two members of security manning the doors because this was a private party. They were probably the ones who found the breaker to bring the lights back, and they would shortly be joined by many more of their colleagues; I knew that for certain. Looking all around still, a heartfelt sob from the centre of the crowd pulled my eyes that way.

'She's dead!' wailed a woman with a Kiwi accent.

I pushed forward, Verity still holding my hand and trailing along behind as I made my way through the crowd to the source of the voice.

A small crowd were gathered on the deck where a pair of feet were sticking out from between the floor-length dresses and dinner jackets.

Howard was running forward from the stage where he had cowered during the shooting. He ran to his wife, his face white with horror at what he might find.

The people parted to let him in, and I saw, just as he did, his wife, Shandy, covered in a slick of blood. It was coming from a bullet wound to her neck, but she was alive. Cradled in her left arm, as she held her right hand to stem the blood coming from her own wound, was her younger sister, Grace.

Grace was quite dead.

The two members of the ship's security were swinging into action. They were both on the radio, calling for assistance, alerting the bridge to the incident, and summoning medical aid. I recognised both men though they were not two I knew by name. They were doing their job, so I left them to get on with it, but unable to stop myself, I got involved.

'Did anyone see the shot or the shooter?' I asked, standing tall and raising my voice to make myself heard.

A ripple of murmurs went around the room, but a man standing just a few feet from me said. 'It was dark. How could anyone see it?' He was another Kiwi, the room had to be half-filled with Shandy's relatives though I knew she had moved to America with Howard many years ago. Americans made up the other half of the crowd with a few odd-ball English like Verity and me thrown in.

His wife, I assumed for she was holding his hand, said, 'I saw it.'

I saw him squeeze her hand; the action painful for his wife if her sudden grimace was any indication. 'No, you didn't, Alice. Don't get involved,' he insisted as he tried to escort her away.

She yanked her hand free, scowling at him for a second as she made her way back to me.

'I saw it too,' said another voice, this time an elderly man. Both he and the lady were Kiwis. 'My wife and I both. It came from somewhere near the stage, but I didn't see who fired it. I didn't see anyone at all.'

'Nor did I,' agreed his wife, 'but the flash of light definitely came in front of where Grace and Shandy were standing.'

I looked at Alice, the first person to have spoken and got a nod from her to confirm that correlated with what she saw.

On the deck, Howard was kneeling at his dead sister-in-law's side and trying to comfort his wife. He was the only one on the stage but, like any stage on the planet, it had access from the sides and from the rear where a curtain fell to conceal what was behind.

I took a second to look around the room. All around me, the party guests were looking stunned and staring inward to the focal point where Shandy, Howard, and Grace were gathered on the deck. Some were crying, others were white as sheets. There was no reason for me to get involved, but hearing Shandy's confession about the stalker earlier, I had to question if my conscience would allow me not to.

The two security guys met for a fast exchange of words, then one held up his hands. 'Ladies and Gentlemen, I am Lieutenant Salman Kumar. I know you have all been witness to a terrible incident, but I must ask that you all remain here at this time.' Mutterings arose from his audience, but he continued speaking. 'It will be necessary to question you all on what you saw.'

'What if I didn't see anything?' The shout drew all eyes to Alice's loudmouth husband who looked mostly bored and made it obvious he had no time to be hanging around. 'There's no need to stay if we didn't see anything,' he stated authoritatively.

Lieutenant Kumar wisely chose to ignore him. 'I assure you we will process and move you all on as swiftly as we are able. As soon as an alternate venue can be located, we will move you all there, but for now, I must insist, ' he accented the word 'insist' hard enough to make sure Alice's husband would understand, 'that you all remain here.' He didn't add a please at the end; it wasn't a request.

The sound of running feet drew my eyes to the main door which the guards had closed to keep the guests corralled inside. They flew open now as a dozen men and women rushed through them. Right at the front was Lieutenant Deepa Bhukari, a woman originally from Pakistan and a person I now considered as a friend. Hard on her heels was the captain, Alistair Huntley, a former lover who was waiting for me to make my mind up about what I wanted from life. The door to his heart was open for me to walk in and stay for as long as I wanted. I couldn't focus on that issue right now because there was a far more pressing and urgent matter at hand.

Lieutenant Kumar wasted no time in delivering his report to the captain who paused to listen while everyone else coming in behind him fanned out and got to work. Dr Kim, his medical bag in hand, was followed a moment later by two orderlies with a gurney on wheels.

The doctor made a beeline for the obvious crowd around the victims still lying on the deck and I went with him. Until now, getting any closer felt like I would be intruding. Now though, I was able to justify my involvement by assisting the doctor because I knew the victims.

'Mrs Fisher,' Dr Kim acknowledged me as he came to kneel by Grace's body.

The bullet had struck her forehead, leaving no question she might still be alive. Dr Kim motioned for his orderlies to cover her body and coaxed Shandy to let her sister go.

'I need to treat your wound,' he insisted softly.

Her right hand was still clamped on the right side of her neck where blood ran between her fingers and down her arm. One thing I believed for certain was that she was lucky to be alive. The bullet must have come close to opening the artery supplying her head.

'It was supposed to be me,' Shandy wailed as Howard did his best to pull his wife's left arm away from her sister. Shandy didn't want to let Grace go and was howling and screaming as Howard tried to make her release the body. 'It's my fault!' she cried, huge wracking sobs shaking her whole body.

She was talking about the stalker, of course. It seemed everyone in the room knew about it; I had heard many of them muttering and discussing the subject since the moment the lights came back on. If she received a hand-delivered note today, then the stalker was on board with them and that was a scary thought. Why hadn't they done something about it though? Were the security team even aware of the threat? Had they known, surely there would have been more of them here?

On the deck, Dr Kim was attempting to get a look at Shandy's wound but her hand was clamped to her neck and she was fighting him off. 'No!' she screamed. 'Take me out of here! I can feel the blood under my hand. I'm not moving it!'

'It's all right, Mrs Berkowitz,' Dr Kim used a soothing voice, attempting to calm the irrational and panicked woman. 'I need to treat your wound. The artery cannot be compromised; the bleeding would be far worse if it were.' He reached out to take her hand away from the wound again and she slapped him away.

'No!' she screamed again. 'Howard, I want to leave. Please make them take me out of here.'

Dr Kim nodded to the two medics who came with him. They had a portable stretcher with fold-out wheels. It was in its collapsed state so with a little help from Howard and the medics, Shandy schooched across the deck and onto it.

Dr Kim asked the crowd to part so they could leave and said, 'We'll treat your wound in the sickbay, Mrs Berkowitz.' He was being tolerant and patient, skills I was sure any doctor needed to deal with the emotional people they must meet every day.

They were about to depart but Shandy was refusing to leave her sister's body on the floor, so they were waiting for another stretcher to collect Grace first. Shandy's hand was still clamped tightly to her neck.

I spotted Alistair and rushed over to speak with him. It was his ship – well, technically it was Purple Cruise Lines' ship, but he was the captain – and he needed to manage what came next. I felt sure the Berkowitzs would have no choice other than to tell his team about the stalker since I was sure they hadn't done so yet. However, letting him know now would get the ball rolling. We were at dock, so the killer could be trying to sneak off the ship at this very moment.

'No, I had all the exits shut the moment Kumar informed the bridge,' Alistair told me. 'I can't keep them closed forever, of course, and when I say closed; we are still letting people back on board. The killer is, however, still on the ship somewhere.'

I told him about the stalker and the emails and letter, passing on what I knew even though it wasn't much. He nodded along as he listened and when I finished, I looked up into his beautiful eyes and said, 'I can be involved if you want me to be. Or I can stay out of it; you tell me, Alistair.' I was being generous. Usually, I just inserted myself into the investigations on board the ship whether I was invited or not, but before he could answer me, Howard Berkowitz grabbed my shoulder.

The suddenness of it startled me. 'Sorry,' he apologised. 'I have to go with Shandy now.'

Alistair inclined his head toward the billionaire. 'I am so sorry for your loss, sir.'

Howard's bottom lip wobbled. 'It's … it's all so terrible.' He shook his head to clear it, took a deep breath and fixed his eyes on me. 'Mrs Fisher, I want to hire you to find Grace's killer.'

'That's not fair to her,' called Shandy from her stretcher. They were just getting ready to take her away and looked to be waiting for Howard more than anything. 'Patricia is here on vacation.'

'I can pay you handsomely,' he begged. 'Name your price. That bullet was meant for my Shandy.'

'Mr Berkowitz, we really have to take your wife to sickbay now,' Dr Kim implored Howard to stop delaying them.

He twitched his head in their direction, and back at me as he started to move away. 'Please, Patricia. Anything you want. I'll buy you the ship if that's what it takes. No money in the world can replace what we have lost today.' He had to raise his voice as he neared the doors. 'The killer may strike again, Mrs Fisher! Solve the mystery and find Grace's murderer before he can take anyone else from me.'

His final words echoed through the ballroom, reverberating off the walls and ceiling so that everyone in the room heard him.

Alistair leaned his head down to whisper in my ear. 'Try getting out of it now.'

Lieutenants Baker, Schneider, Bhukari, and Pippin were assigned to me by Alistair upon my request. If I was going to try to find the killer, I wanted a team at my side. Merely thinking about my team made my mind jump to Jermaine and Barbie, the two people closest to me and ones who could almost be called sidekicks.

It wasn't either of them who found me amidst the chaos at the start of the investigation though. It was Agent Wayne Garrett, who barrelled into the room, fighting with the security guard placed at the front entrance of the ballroom as Wayne tried to get in and the guard attempted to keep him out.

Agent Garrett is a policeman from a special branch of Scotland Yard dedicated to investigating organised crime. He was assigned to keep me alive while the Godmother threat remained, but truly, I believed he was close to me so he could watch for signs of activity that might lead his department back to her. Either way, he was sworn to remain by my side, and it had taken a lot of convincing to leave him in the suite this evening so I could attend the party without him.

I might never hear the end of it.

Lieutenant Schneider indicated that Agent Garrett should be let through and the guard on the door relented.

'Mrs Fisher, you are unharmed?' Wayne enquired once he was within earshot.

I guess his concerned face was due to the pool of blood he could see just a few feet from me. 'I am fine,' I assured him. 'Shots were fired. A woman, the host's sister-in-law, was killed and his wife was injured though not badly enough that her life is in danger.' The information did little to please him. 'I was not the target,' I added.

'For once,' he grumbled under his breath. 'I hope, Mrs Fisher, that you will not argue when I insist on accompanying you everywhere except the ladies' restrooms which I will, however, be searching before you go inside.'

I rolled my eyes and dismissed about ten responses I deemed unusable. Unable to come up with a response, I let it go – I had more important tasks to distract me. On my request, a plan of the room was being drawn up and the relative position of every guest at the time of the shooting was being marked on it. Baker's team of security guards were taking statements from every guest and asking people to send them all the photographs they had taken at the party – the killer might be in one of them.

With a few more questions, and after several more people had come forward to state they saw the muzzle flash from the stage, we were able to roughly identify the position where the shot had been taken. It was just in front of the stage and close to where Howard had been standing. The killer could have rushed out from the left or right side of the stage, taken the shot, and vanished again. Or could conceivably have run out from the crowd, turned, and fired. If the stalker was in the room, would the Berkowitzs recognise who it was? Shandy said she didn't know their stalker's identity, but could it be someone they knew? Had they, unwittingly invited the killer to the party? Given how many were attending, the killer could have snuck in among the guests, but my initial gut reaction was to believe they had been waiting in the wings and struck when they turned off the lights.

The two ejected shell casings were found in seconds when the team started looking for them. They had both fetched up against the bottom lip of a tall potted plant at the edge of the stage. Being thorough, Alistair's security detachment sent for a crime scene kit. Since they had to act as police, detectives, crime scene investigators and even jailers at times, they had a wide spread of skills. They wanted to swab for gun shot residue but knew most of the expelled chemical particles would have coated the shooter. It would be on the killer's hands and clothing. There were trace amounts on the deck, but so far as evidence went, the crime scene was almost bare.

Most of the guests had been corralled to the exit/entrance end of the ballroom well away from the scene of the shooting and then, when one of the upper deck bars could be cleared, the remainder were moved there until they could be interviewed. Speaking with everyone was a formality: there was no good reason to suspect anyone at the party. Many of the guests had been flown in from America or New Zealand specially for the event by the Berkowitzs and were supposed to be enjoying the next leg of the Aurelia's trip since the party was supposed to have occurred at sea.

Then I spotted a flaw in my logic. I was assuming the killer and the stalker were one and the same. The threats, which I had yet to see for myself, had all been emails until the letter this morning. At least, I believed that to be the case. I needed to confirm it, but the killer was not necessarily the one who sent the threatening emails or the hand-delivered note.

It was coming up on midnight and I wanted to get to bed. A yawn split my face to prove the point and Lieutenant Schneider sidled up to me as I tried to wrestle my face back under control. Verity had long since departed, shooed away by me because she didn't need to be party to all that was going to happen in the aftermath of the shooting

When I could finally look at Schneider again, he said, 'We can carry on here, Mrs Fisher. There is plenty for us to be doing. Perhaps by the morning, Mrs Berkowitz will be able to answer some questions.' Baker spoke with Dr Kim a few minutes ago to check on her condition only to discover she had been transferred to a hospital in Reykjavik.

Part of me wanted to stay behind, but I knew this would go on all night. Like anyone, I need to sleep, and I still hadn't managed to eat anything much since the rest of the canapes never arrived. When another yawn threatened to force my mouth open again, I patted Schneider on his muscular arm and waved goodnight. Alistair, and the surplus members of the security team had already departed, getting some sleep themselves so they would be fresh in the morning. The crime scene was just about packed up, but Schneider was hanging on for the engineering team to work out how or why the lights had gone out. It had to have been deliberate – the killer had reacted too fast for the lights to have gone out by accident, and we wanted to see how the killer did it. While his colleagues got to go to bed, Lieutenant Schneider had drawn the short straw it seemed.

Agent Garrett, who spent a lot of his time silently hanging around and watching for danger, hadn't exactly been taxed for the last couple of hours. He said nothing about being kept up late but looked ready to retire when I started moving toward the door.

'Terrible way to go,' he commented, then glanced my way to see how I might react. To my raised eyebrow he added, 'Accidentally, I mean. If the bullet really was meant for Mrs Berkowitz, and her sister was killed instead, I understand that is what happened, then I cannot think of a worse fate.'

I mulled that over for a second. 'There was no time to suffer. I think maybe that is something I would hope for: a painless death.'

Agent Garrett nodded. 'I guess you are right. What would be your worst way to go?'

It was a macabre line of enquiry but rather than demand a change of subject, he was just making conversation, I played along. 'Eaten by a shark maybe.' I thought some more. 'Perhaps my answer should be dying alone. I have known people who grew old and had to watch everyone they knew, the friends and relatives, die first. Something sudden, like what happened to Grace, that would be preferable to burying everyone else one at a time.' I was starting to freak myself out. 'Look, can we change the subject, please?'

Agent Garrett bowed his head. 'Of course. My apologies. Shall I message ahead to have Jermaine fix up a gin and tonic, Mrs Fisher?' he asked as he fell into step next to me.

I would have answered with a definite yes, please if Alistair hadn't chosen that very moment to appear.

'Might I join you for a nightcap?' the captain enquired.

Respectfully, Agent Garrett dropped back a pace so I could walk with Alistair instead. I offered the captain a smile, and he offered me his arm. Together, we walked back to my suite, and in that moment, as arm in arm we felt no need to talk, a cog clicked into place and a decision got made.

Approaching the door to my suite, I used my free hand to rummage in my handbag for my keycard. Agent Garrett darted around me with his but even he didn't get to open the door for it magically swung inward as I came within six feet of it.

It wasn't magic, of course, but my tall, Jamaican butler, Jermaine. I loved Jermaine with all my heart in a completely platonic way. The message from Agent Garrett had been sent anyway, alerting the man waiting inside my suite that Agent Garrett, the captain, and I were on route.

My two dachshunds came bouncing out of the door to greet me. Anna, a shaded red bitch I came by through fate or perhaps serendipity while I was in Tokyo, and Georgie, her daughter who was a dachshund cross corgi, not that she looked any different from her mother, were inseparable. Georgie is still a puppy whose age can be measured in months using one hand. She entered a chewing stage recently which has me a little worried because I am staying in a grand suite where everything is insanely expensive.

I unhooked my arm from Alistair's, scooped one under each arm, and kissed their heads on my way through the door.

'Good evening, madam,' Jermaine dipped his head regally. 'Good evening, Captain Huntley.' He held the door open for us and closed it once we were inside, then took the captain's hat when it was offered. I thought I saw an exchange of glances between Jermaine and Agent Garrett and knew I was right when Wayne bade me a good night and vanished into his room – they were clearing out to give us some privacy.

My suite has several bedrooms. Enough to fit Barbie, Wayne, me, and my housemaid from England, Molly, in and for there to still be a spare bed left over. To describe my surroundings as opulent is to miss the point. It is the world's most luxurious cruise liner and I am staying in the royal suite. Some days I was surprised there wasn't a champagne tap made of gold in the kitchen.

'Might I prepare you a beverage, madam?' Jermaine asked. 'Or perhaps a light snack?'

My belly complained loudly at the suggestion of food, but it was late, and Jermaine deserved to get some downtime. 'Thank you, Jermaine. I think tonight I will just see to myself.'

He dipped his head once more. 'Very good, madam.' Normally he would have argued and insisted it was his pleasure to bring me whatever I desired, but he sensed the captain and I wanted to be alone, so, like Agent Garrett, he bade us both a goodnight and departed through the door in the kitchen which led to his adjoining cabin.

Now we were alone, I knew what I wanted to do and what I wanted to say, but I moved into the kitchen area of my suite first – I needed a drink.

'Gin?' I asked Alistair, taking a bottle of ice-cold Hendricks from the freezer, and holding it up for him to see.

He slid onto one of the bar stools on the opposite side of the kitchen worktop and shot me a grin. 'You read my mind, Patricia.'

I busied myself making two gin and tonics knowing I would be making two more shortly. The fatigue I felt just before leaving the ballroom was gone, replaced by an itch of excitement in my core. I was controlling our relationship, I always had once it got started, but Alistair appeared content to let me steer so long as we arrived at the correct destination.

I passed him a large balloon glass filled with swirling clear liquid, ice, and cucumber, lifted mine in a salute and took a good slug from it. The heady botanicals washed over my tastebuds, cleansing my palette, and awakening an altogether different hunger to the one in my stomach.

Eyeing Alistair carefully, just as he had been eyeing me appreciatively since Jermaine left the room. I swirled my glass, took another sip, and placed it down on the counter. I had been trying to play it cool, but the time for that was now past.

I plucked the glass from his hand before he could get it to his lips. It would have been in the way there, and as his questioning look turned up toward me, I grabbed his shirt and pulled his face to mine.

Fooling Nobody

I awoke a little after three in the morning to the sound of Alistair dressing. It was gone midnight when we arrived back at my suite and we hadn't gotten a lot of sleep in the intervening couple of hours. I don't want to make comparisons with putting on an old comfortable shirt or other suitable garment that fits the analogy, but being back with Alistair, that was exactly how it felt.

We hadn't split up when I left the Aurelia. At the time, our lives were on different trajectories and I felt an undeniable, irresistible need to strike out on my own. The itch I needed to scratch then didn't feel as itchy now as it had at the time and since the moment I saw him again just over a week ago, my desire to kiss and hold him had been growing.

Right now, lying in bed as I watched him buttoning up his shirt, I knew I would struggle to articulate, even to myself, why I had felt the need to resist him and keep him at arm's length. Choosing to allow the relationship to rekindle wasn't without obstacles; he was still never going to leave the ship and I wasn't sure about a life on board one as his significant other. I wasn't about to marry Alistair and prayed he wasn't going to propose. I had been married for thirty years and still was, my ridiculous husband dragging the procedure of divorce out as he tried desperately to get his hands on money that he had no right to claim.

Alistair donned his jacket and noticed that I was watching him. His face softened and he knelt on the bed to kiss me. 'I thought you were asleep.'

'And you were just going to sneak out,' I accused him jokingly.

He kissed me again and left the bed. 'Well ...'

He was going to say something cutting about not wanting to buy the cow once you'd drunk the milk but whatever he was going to say got cut off when my pillow hit his face.

He danced away chuckling.

'Get out, you scurvy pirate,' I insisted.

He gave me his twinkling eyes, the ones that melted my heart and my will every time, and with one hand on the door handle, he said, 'Sleep well, my princess. I will see you in a few hours, I hope.'

Then he was gone. When I lured him to my room, I already knew he couldn't stay the night. His second in command, Commander Ochi was on shore leave with his family whom he'd flown out to meet him. It was only supposed to be for two days but with the ship stuck in dock for repairs, Alistair insisted the man spend as long as he could with his wife and children. The result, obviously, was Alistair picking up double shifts. He would get some of the time back later but, for now, he needed to report to the bridge and replace whoever the current duty watch commander was.

I settled back onto my pillows and fell promptly asleep, waking to the smell of coffee filtering through to my room. I had to flail around a little to fight my way out of the covers, and I had no idea what time it was, but coffee meant someone was in the kitchen and, to my empty stomach, that meant it was breakfast time!

'Hey, Patty,' said Barbie, looking up from behind the kitchen counter where she was doing something with a blender and a whole load of green stuff. 'You want one?' she asked.

My right eyebrow rose all by itself. 'What even is it?'

'Kale, spinach, avocado, and lemon grass smoothy. I add ginger and sriracha to make it a little spicy and that boosts my metabolism which helps me burn more calories,' she explained. Barbie is a gym nut. She lives for the deep aching muscle burn one gets from prolonged or intense exercise and consequently she looks like an Olympic athlete. She had long, straight blonde hair most women would kill for, a figure every woman would kill for, and gravity defying breasts men would kill to get their hands on. She was also most of six feet tall, tanned, and beautiful with a who-needs-makeup flawless complexion that made me want to slap her every time she smiled.

I bit my lip. The smoothy sounded awful, but I was conscious that Barbie's dietary tips were solid gold so when she poured a tiny amount into a glass for me to try, I went ahead and chugged it.

I gave it a second, waiting for my own tastebuds to reject the concoction but, in all honesty, I had tasted much worse things. It tasted very … green. That was for certain, but ginger was coming through as the dominant flavour.

'I'll take a small glass, please.' Barbie dutifully poured me a glass of the green goop, added a couple of ice cubes, and slid it across the counter towards my hand. I continued to look at it sceptically. 'I feel like I am missing out on bacon.'

The glass was in my hand, halfway to my mouth when Barbie put her index finger underneath it and pushed it the rest of the way. 'You can have bacon, Patty. Just trim the fat from it before you eat it and make sure you serve the bacon with veggies and some eggs.'

What? No pancakes and Texas toast? It was like she spoke a different language.

Committing to the concept, I started to drink the smoothie, but when Barbie said, 'What time did Alistair leave?' with a knowing smile on her face. I coughed and choked and spat out twenty percent of it.

Staring at her with green stuff dripping from my lips and nose, I asked, 'How?'

She got what I meant. 'I found two glasses on the counter when I came into the kitchen this morning, Patty. Neither had been finished and that's not like you. Two glasses equals two people. Two unfinished glasses means the two people found something more interesting to do than finish their drinks. I suppose it might not necessarily be Alistair, but I'd be willing to bet that it was.'

I gave her a lopsided smile. What else could I do? 'It was Alistair,' I admitted with not the slightest tinge of guilt. Barbie and I were a generation apart, but we were both women and our desires and needs in life were not dissimilar.

She met my eyes with a level stare. 'I think you made the right decision,' she told me, making it clear she believed every word. Thankfully, I agreed. Then in a quiet voice tinged with sadness, she said, 'I miss Hideki.'

I reached out to place my hand on top of hers. 'Are you getting to speak to him much?'

Her right shoulder twitched with a half shrug. 'I guess. Here and there when we can. It's not the same, of course, and I think he is unhappy that I cannot tell him when I will be coming back to England.' Looking irritated at voicing her glumness, she picked up her bottle of green stuff and checked her watch. 'I had better get going.'

'You're on your way to the gym?' I asked, skipping forward to a new subject.

'Yes.' She chugged half of her green smoothie. 'I want to get in a workout before I have my own class.'

'What time is it?' I asked, squinting at the clock on the oven.

Her answer surprised me. 'Five after six.'

'What! What on Earth am I doing out of bed?'

She laughed at me. 'I expect the release of endorphins a few hours ago has caused a spike in your alertness. I figured you knew how early it was. Why do you think Jermaine isn't up yet?'

I was going to pay for the early start later when the lack of sleep caught up with me, but I wasn't going to go back to bed. As Barbie finished the last of her smoothy and washed the glass out in the sink, I started to think about the Berkowitzs and their stalker. This morning, I was going to have to ask them some pointed questions and get to the bottom of why they were being stalked.

First though, I was going to take myself for a little jog around the ship. It would do the dogs good to get some exercise and though it was early, I felt sure the person in cabin 34782 would forgive me for rousing them.

The Person in Cabin 34782

I had to use my own money to book the cabin on deck eight but convincing the person now inside the suite to come on this trip had been easier than I thought. I ran for half an hour first which was mostly because I wanted to be doubly sure I wasn't being followed. It might have been paranoia, but I needed to be certain the person inside the cabin on deck eight remained a secret.

A little out of breath, I arrived at the door marked 34782 just before seven o'clock which didn't sound all that early to be waking someone if they were indeed still asleep. Continuing my cautious approach, I waited in the passageway for over a minute, glancing left and right to make sure no one else was around before I knocked on the door.

Finally content I was alone, I rapped my knuckles on the wood, and waited.

Anna and Georgie knew a door when they saw one and were facing it with their noses almost pressed against the wood. I guess in a dog's head there might be anything on the other side, but almost certainly there would be a person and that generally meant being made a fuss of. But also, there could be food and that was worth investigating.

The noise of someone moving on the other side was replaced a moment later by the sound of the door being unlocked. Then it swung open, my right hand surging forward as both dogs ran into the cabin, pulling on their leads as they went.

The person looking out at me was already dressed and set for the day. 'Good morning, Patricia.'

I smiled in return. 'Good morning, Mike.'

Inside his cabin, I settled at the small table and two chairs set next to the porthole window. The dogs were off their leads and sniffing their way around the space looking for crumbs of food. Mike Atwell is a detective sergeant with the Kent police and the local detective covering my village. He and I got to know each other when I returned home from my previous trip and started my own private investigation business. He was my big secret on board the Aurelia, a set of eyes and ears that no one else knew about.

'So, what do you think?' I asked. 'Am I right?'

He puffed out his cheeks to show he wasn't sure and said, 'I cannot tell yet. You might be. I need more time, but yes, the Godmother might very well already have agents on board.'

I let my head drop. It was my worst fears coming true. My escape to the Aurelia was supposed to be about buying time. The Godmother wanted me dead for what she considered past insults and there seemed no way of stopping her or convincing her to give up on her quest for my head. It was a matter of honour, it seemed. I had insulted her by attacking or damaging her organisation on three occasions, not that I had done so knowingly, and she needed to balance the scales by ending my life.

'I came here to give myself a little breathing space,' I complained.

'But you knew well enough to bring me along, Patricia,' Mike pointed out. 'You knew she might infiltrate the police and be able to intercept or decode any messages to know your plans. The question now is what can you do about it?'

I snorted a wry laugh. 'I've put everyone on board in danger.'

Mike didn't disagree, but he said, 'But the people around you would be in danger no matter where you were. You are the one who dangled the lure.'

Mike was right. I chose to intentionally leave a clue to my whereabouts on my business website hinting that I had returned to the Aurelia. I expected it to take the Godmother longer to get someone on board, but it wasn't someone I was after. I wanted her here. Unfortunately, it meant bringing everyone on board into harm's way and now I felt guilty for doing so.

I blew out a hard breath and reset my brain. I had a case to solve with the Berkowitzs stalker/killer, and I would get to that shortly. It couldn't have my full attention though because I also had to reel in the much bigger fish.

'Okay,' I said standing up. 'You will continue to observe?'

He nodded. 'It is why I am here. This was your trap, Patricia. You suspected the Godmother would send someone closer to her this time, not just hired assassins. Everyone I have looked into so far has checked out as you know. However, if her people are here, and if they attempt to get to know you, or are clearly observing you, I will find them and then find out who they are.

That was part one of the plan. An underworld figure shrouded in mystery, the Godmother had proved impossible to identify, let alone catch despite years of police work committed to the task. The Alliance of Families – the police had at least found out what her organisation called itself – was a global player in organised crime. Sitting at the top of it was the Godmother who unified the effort of crime families around the world to prevent arguments over turf and wasted effort fighting each other when their efforts could be turned to profit.

If she wanted me dead, she would send people to the Aurelia and they would make the mistake of speaking to me at some point. I believed that wholeheartedly. Mike was watching, and anyone who came close to me was getting a full background check using his contacts back home in England. If I could identify them, maybe I could use that to track my way back to her. Identifying who she was didn't solve the case though. In order to be free of her, I needed to make sure her whole organisation fell and for that I needed evidence, not just of crime, but of the global movement of money, drugs, people, guns and anything else they might be up to.

Sounds easy, doesn't it? Ha! The worst part was that while I tried to catch her without her knowing I had any idea her people were here, I also needed to avoid getting killed.

I might think of myself as the mongoose staring down the cobra. But does the mongoose always win?

My Assistant

On my way back to my suite, I stopped off on deck nineteen to knock for Sam. I almost messaged him last night when the investigation got started but it was already around bedtime and I didn't want to disturb his parents, Melissa and Paul. Sam Chalk is my thirty-year-old assistant. He has Downs Syndrome, which affects his cognitive ability, yet he sees things I don't, he is permanently positive and always smiling, and just a treasure to spend time with. He needed a job and I needed some company that wasn't a sausage dog.

He took a bullet to his left shoulder when we caught the man sabotaging the Aurelia and his arm was still in a sling. His mother was keeping quiet about how freaked out she was by his injury even though he loved telling people he got shot. I felt I was lucky she hadn't tried to throttle me yet.

Melissa opened her door, peering around the edge of the frame cautiously as if unsure who could be knocking. 'Oh, hi, Patricia,' her expression changed to a pleasant smile. 'Is this a social call or are you here for Sam?'

'Mostly for Sam,' I admitted. I chose to invite them along on this trip because I was scared the Godmother might choose to target them due to their association with me. Sam's parents were having a great time though and I was their favourite person in the world, not just because they got a holiday for free, but because I gave Sam a job and a purpose when no one else would.

'Hi, Mrs Fisher,' said Sam, looking up from watching cartoons on the couch in their suite. 'I've got a girlfriend.'

'Good morning, Sam,' I replied automatically, though I was looking at Melissa for confirmation. I mouthed, 'Girlfriend?'

Melissa grinned and flipped her eyebrows as if it were a joke. 'He met another girl with Downs a couple of days ago. They hit it off and have been on a couple of dates.' She made air quotes when she said the word 'dates', then explained, 'They went out for dinner and to one of the shows. It's all quite innocent. I would love for him to have a more normal life. He already does since you gave him a job, but ... well, you know what I mean. Anyway, she's twenty-five and she's American which makes her exotic as far as Sam is concerned. Unfortunately, she's also leaving with her parents when the ship gets to Dublin (our next stop after Iceland) and I think he might be a little heartbroken when she does.'

I had to feel sorry for Melissa. She wanted so many things for Sam that were simply out of reach. For the most part, he acted blissfully unaware of the things he missed out on, but perhaps she was right about the sting of love lost. Wouldn't we all rather avoid that one?

The dogs were pulling at their leads to go inside and explore but I needed to get a shower and a proper breakfast. 'I won't come in,' I let the Chalks know. 'I just stopped by to let Sam know we have a case.'

'Another one?' Melissa sounded surprised.

I pulled a face. 'There was a murder last night.'

Her mouth formed a shocked 'O'. But when Sam whooped his delight, it switched immediately to a hard frown. 'Samuel Chalk, we do not celebrate other people being murdered, thank you very much.'

I backed out of the doorway. 'I'll see you in my suite in an hour, okay?'

Sam had quashed his joy at hearing we had a murder to investigate, but it returned instantly. 'I'll bring my magnifying glass,' he let me know. His magnifying glass, the first one anyway, was at the bottom of the ocean, but he'd bought a new one the moment they got off the ship in Reykjavik. He felt it was a necessary part of his uniform for sleuthing and took it everywhere. At no point had his last one ever come in useful, but I wasn't going to dampen his enthusiasm, no, sir.

In my suite, I let the dogs off their lead, watching them both scamper away toward the kitchen where Jermaine was preparing food. Molly was sitting on the couch reading a magazine. The smells coming from the kitchen clearly held more interest for the dogs than the likelihood of cuddles with the teenage housemaid.

'Morning, Mrs Fisher,' said Molly without looking up. She was curled into one corner of the couch with her bare feet tucked beneath her and a cup of tea sat steaming by her arm where it rested on a side table. 'One of those Lieutenants came by looking for you just a few minutes ago.'

'Good morning, Molly. Which one was it, please?' I asked.

She looked up from the all-engrossing magazine with a quizzical expression. She didn't know and hadn't thought to ask for their name.

'It was Lieutenant Baker, madam,' Jermaine supplied from the kitchen before I had to go through a description to get the answer from Molly.

'Yeah,' Molly agreed. 'The old one.' Martin Baker was about thirty. Hardly old by anyone's standards but was probably the eldest in the group.

'Breakfast, madam?' Jermaine enquired.

Before I could answer, Agent Garrett appeared from his room. He offered me a stern expression and accentuated it by folding his arms in a manner that suggested he was displeased. I knew why. Yet again, I snuck out without telling him. He was supposed to be my bodyguard, and with me at all times. Losing him to visit Mike was becoming more and more difficult and he was becoming increasingly suspicious of my need to do so. Soon, I would be forced to communicate with Mike Atwell by phone only, and it would have to be the ship's internal phone system too so my calls would not be logged on my mobile.

I waved a guilty hand at him to acknowledge I was in the wrong. 'I know, I know. I just wanted to go for a jog without having someone running along behind me. Nothing happened, did it,' I pointed out though I knew that wasn't the point.

His expression didn't change. 'A woman was murdered last night, Mrs Fisher.'

Molly looked up suddenly. 'Really?'

I nodded. 'Yes. At the party I attended. The sister of the hostess was shot. They think it might have been the hostess the shooter was aiming at. I am yet to start the investigation.'

'Cor, you're going to investigate it?' she asked. Then she pursed her lips and looked like she wanted to ask a question. 'Can I help?' she enquired.

Her question got a raised eyebrow from all three of us. If the dachshunds understood the question, they might have raised their eyebrows too, or whatever the canine equivalent to a raised eyebrow is. Molly had barely moved since we came aboard. She went to the pool and read books or magazines. Or she hung out in the room reading or watching television. Like Sam, I chose to bring her along for her own protection, and it was essentially a vacation; she wasn't here as my maid, so I made no comment about her sloth-like behaviour.

'You want to help with the investigation?' I sought to confirm.

She gave a half-hearted shrug. 'This cruising malarkey was fun to start with – ignoring the bit where I almost got killed several times – but it's getting boring now. I was wondering about seeing if there are any jobs going. Anders said he thought there were some openings for the security team.'

Now my other eyebrow joined the first at the top of my forehead. I wasn't aware that she had even met Lieutenant Pippin, let alone that she was on first name terms with him. It shouldn't have surprised me; he can't be more than a couple of years older than her and has been in my suite many times in the last week. They must have bumped into each other at some point and started talking because they recognised each other. Joining the security team … that didn't sound like the Molly I thought I knew.

Forcing my eyebrows back down to their resting position, I said, 'I can ask, if you like. I imagine there will be some training to do.' I wasn't exactly trying to put her off, just throwing a barrier in her way to see if it was enough to make her change her mind.

Instead, she put down the magazine and stood up. 'There is,' she announced. 'I already looked into it. Would you mind?' she asked me.

Now I felt my head tilt to one side. I was about to ask why she was asking my opinion until I remembered that she thought of me as her employer. I wasn't. Not technically, at least. The Maharaja of Zangrabar was since he paid her wages.

I offered her a broad smile. 'I think it's a great idea, Molly.' I wasn't sure what her mother might make of her decision, but Molly wasn't in yet and I believed the selection process to be quite rigorous. She was a young woman with her life ahead of her and why shouldn't she explore the world?

Jermaine had left the kitchen and was waiting patiently for our conversation to conclude so he could prompt me for a decision about breakfast. That wasn't all though, I noticed, when I saw a silver tray in his hand. There was an envelope on it.

At first glance, my heart skipped because I thought it to be a telegram from the Maharaja. It wasn't though, it was just a letter, and when I looked closer, I saw that it was embossed with the logo of my husband's lawyer.

Seeing my face, Jermaine said, 'It arrived while you were out, madam.'

I started muttering as I picked it up. It was postmarked a week ago and had been addressed to me care of Purple Star Cruise Lines. Charlie must have guessed I had returned to the ship despite my cryptic answers. Or maybe it was because of my cryptic answers. Either way, it had found me.

'Jermaine, dear. Could you make me some scrambled egg and smoked salmon, please?'

'Heavy on the dill?' he enquired.

'Yes, please.' He knew how I liked it and returned to the kitchen where he would lay out what he needed and await my return so he could prepare and serve it fresh. I took the letter to my bedroom where I would read it in private and get ready for the day. I also sent a text message to Lieutenant Baker to say I was sorry I missed him and that he could find me now.

Pulling off my running gear, I had a feeling I was in for a busy day.

Who's the Target?

People began to arrive just after I finished my breakfast. The first of them was Lieutenant Mike Baker, a member of the ship's security team who I had a lot of time for. He was a nice person and soon to be wed to Deepa Bhukari, another member of the security detachment. I wanted to ask him about what would happen regards their accommodation after the nuptials but now wasn't the time. Barbie had told me something about it, not that I could remember what she said, but they couldn't be married and expected to share one of the tiny crew cabins way below deck.

He accepted a steaming mug of coffee when Jermaine offered it and sat at the kitchen counter to explain what they had discovered while I was asleep. I asked him to wait until Sam arrived, which he did a few minutes later. We were joined by Agent Wayne Garrett who figured he might as well lend his cop brain to the task since he had to be wherever I was, and by Molly who was apparently quite serious about the security team thing and wanted to see them operate up close.

'The captain reopened the doors this morning for free movement of crew and passengers. Everyone is checked on and off anyway and there were only a small handful of people prevented from leaving the ship last night.'

'Did any of them seem like likely suspects?' I asked. The point of stopping people from leaving wasn't so much to ensure the killer stayed on board; that could only be a temporary fix as the captain would have to open the doors again, but more to see if anyone tried to get off anyway. If the killer were looking for a fast escape, they would have been caught had they attempted to break through security or avoid them by exiting the ship by a different method, like climbing down a mooring rope. Since no one had done anything like that, the killer was either wise enough to play it cool, or possibly had no intention of leaving the ship yet.

Baker shook his head. 'No. It was already late, and I think in total they only had to turn two people away. We received over eight thousand photographs from the various party goers.' Eight thousand! I guess modern phones make it easy to snap happy. 'Deepa and Anders started going through them earlier, but nothing so far. They had a couple of the family members from each side volunteer to help them identify the people in the pictures. They are looking, obviously, for anyone they don't recognise, but … like I said, nothing so far.'

'What else?' I prompted him for more information. 'What about the lights? Did the engineers find something?'

He took an electronic notepad from a trouser pocket, reading from it rather than relying on memory as I might try to do. 'Indeed, they did. It took them a while, but someone had fitted a device that overloaded the lighting circuit. It was remote operated so whoever fitted it could operate it from a phone or other device.'

'Was it something anyone could buy?' Wayne asked.

Baker shook his head. 'It was homemade, and technical. Whoever built it, knew what they were doing.' He looked at his notes again. 'The rounds used were 9mm; we can tell that much from the shell casings, but we found the bullet that narrowly missed killing Mrs Berkowitz.'

'Where was it?' asked Agent Garrett.

Baker swung his head to look in Wayne's direction when he answered. 'Embedded between two panels where it looked like all the other screw holes around it. It was a 9mm parabellum round.'

Wayne gave a sad snort. 'The most common handgun round on the planet and used in over half of the world's handguns.'

Lieutenant Baker looked just as disappointed. 'It is, at least, intact which ought to mean it can be matched to the murder weapon if we are able to find it.'

'Couldn't someone just throw it overboard?' asked Molly, miming a person opening their porthole and dropping something out.

Baker nodded that she was right. 'That's why we have a team of divers beneath the ship searching to see if someone did exactly that.'

'That's a big area to search,' I observed.

Baker didn't argue, he said, 'The ship is not going anywhere for a while. Mrs Berkowitz was transferred to the hospital in Reykjavik during the night. Dr Kim said it wasn't necessary when I spoke with him, but Mr Berkowitz insisted it seems. I guess money has its uses because Mr Berkowitz had a plastic surgeon flown across Iceland from a hospital on the other side of the country just to look at his wife's neck.'

'Did you get to question them?' I asked.

Lieutenant Baker shook his head and it was clear from his expression that he wasn't happy about it. Mrs Berkowitz wasn't in any state, emotionally, or physically to answer any questions, and Mr Berkowitz wasn't in the sickbay when I got there.'

'Where was he?' I wanted to know.

Baker was frowning when he said, 'He claimed to need medication for an existing heart condition; the shock had made him feel … off. That was the word he used. He didn't have it with him when he returned, of course, he had taken it and left the packet in his room I guess.'

Agent Garrett picked up on Baker's tone. 'You sound like you don't believe him.'

Baker continued to frown and wiggled his lips as he thought about his response. 'He seemed nervous when he returned. It was like he'd been doing something wrong and was trying to convince me he hadn't been even though I didn't ask him about it. Anyway,' he dropped his frown, 'I tried to ask him about their stalker and who it might be and why they hadn't thought to tell us about the hand-delivered message, but he seemed evasive.'

'Evasive,' Sam echoed.

I think Sam was asking what the word meant but Baker took it that he was asking him to expand. 'Every time I tried to raise the subject, he would hold his hand up to stop me so he could check his phone or make a phone call. He reminded me more than once that running a billion-dollar company takes a lot of effort. When he didn't use his business as an excuse, he would ask Dr Kim about his wife or brush me off because he wanted to check on Mrs Berkowitz. Before I knew it, an ambulance was coming to take them to hospital. I had to hammer home the idea that they would not be allowed to just fly home and he would have to speak with me today. Mrs Berkowitz kept talking about packing their things and leaving as soon as they could.'

'Can you hold them here while the investigation takes place?' Wayne asked.

'I can, actually. The crime took place on board the ship which places them under Bahamian jurisdiction because that is where the ship is registered.' I saw Molly screw her face up and held up a finger to let her know I would explain about international marine law and how it applies to cruise ships later. 'I hope I won't have to confiscate their passports but ...'

When he failed to finish his sentence, we all strained our ears in his direction, waiting for the next word, but after a few seconds, I had to push him. 'But what?'

He pursed his lips and skewed them to one side, looking at me as he tried to work out what he wanted to say. 'But I couldn't help the feeling that he was hiding something, or deliberately not saying something. Like I just said, he was evasive.' He sucked on his lips in thought again. 'Only I didn't see it as that at the time. I thought he was just jittery from shock. Mrs Berkowitz was inconsolable; she really took her sister's death hard. I thought he was trying to be strong for her and part of that was keeping me at arm's length.'

'You don't think that anymore.' I put words in his mouth.

Again, he took his time before answering. 'I'm not sure. Deepa and Pippin went to check the suite on deck nineteen that Mrs Berkowitz's sister Grace Snoke is ... was staying in. There were items missing.'

That got my attention. 'Such as?'

'A laptop for starters. They found the charging lead for it but the computer itself is absent and its whereabouts are unknown. We also failed to find her phone. That's Miss Snoke's phone, I should clarify. She didn't have it about her person when we searched her handbag and there was no trace of it in the room, but yet again, we found the charging cable. I had a team in her room dusting for prints.'

I sat back in my chair to absorb what Lieutenant Baker had just revealed. I voiced my thoughts out loud. 'We were assuming Grace was the unintended victim of an attempted murder. If that is true, why would someone want to steal her phone and computer?'

Lieutenant Baker nodded his head; glad I had arrived on the same page. 'Exactly. There is something going on with the Berkowitzs. I managed to ask Mr Berkowitz about the threatening letters you mentioned. He promised to forward them from his emails, but he is yet to do so. Visiting them both in hospital this morning is high on my list of things to do.'

I finished my coffee, a hot dark brew Jermaine always made just right, and set the mug back onto the counter as I gathered my thoughts.

Molly looked my way. 'What happens now, Mrs Fisher?'

I swivelled my bar stool around and stepped down, checking my clothes were straight as I did. 'Now we start to investigate,' I told her. 'There is a big, fat mystery to unravel and the first thing we need to work out is whether Mrs Berkowitz was the intended victim or not.'

'Why's that our first job?' Molly wanted to know, hurrying to finish her drink so she could be ready to go with me wherever I was going.'

'Because, if the killer was aiming at her and missed, it's likely they will try again.'

It was a measure of whether I had made the right decision about Alistair or not that I still felt good about it now. Kissing him last night, and what followed, had been a conscious choice, but also one driven by desire, a touch of loneliness, and an undeniable sense that the clock was ticking and he would only wait so long before he decided I was just messing him around.

It hadn't been a heat of the moment thing though. I had been keeping him at arm's length for more than a week while I wrestled with my emotions. Having given in to my heart, I held no regret that Alistair was back into my life. There was still a stack of unanswered questions regarding what happens next, but I was ignoring them for the moment.

Back in my bedroom to put in my earrings and grab gloves, hat, and scarf, I couldn't help but feel the presence of the letter from Charlie's lawyers. I had opened it and read it through twice and decided to delay reacting to it for as long as I could.

The content of the letter made me angry. Partially it was the lawyer speak that upset me: it was cold and bold and official. Mostly though it was the insistence that everything I now had was up for grabs and Charlie expected to obtain half of it. They had set a meeting for me to attend in a few weeks' time. I didn't have to go; they couldn't make me, or I could send a lawyer to represent me, but for now I was just going to ignore it. Whatever happened, I wasn't going to let Charlie have half of the mansion in West Malling. He wasn't getting half the cars. I didn't want him to have half of anything.

Much like the Godmother case, I needed to focus on the divorce and deal with it, but it wasn't going to make it to the top of my to do list today. Probably not tomorrow either.

The others were politely waiting for me in the main area of my suite and it wouldn't do to keep them any longer than was necessary. It also wouldn't do to bore them with the nonsense going on in my private life so I pushed it right down, took a second to practice my neutral expression in the mirror – the one where it looked like nothing was bothering me, and left my bedroom and the annoying letter from Charlie behind.

I had quite an entourage today. With Molly tagging along, I had three civilians, plus the four uniformed members of the security team and I knew both Barbie and Jermaine would leap to join me at the slightest hint of a request for their assistance.

Though I always felt safest with Jermaine by my side, I didn't need him today and Wayne Garrett had proven himself to be a worthy bodyguard, throwing himself in front of a bullet to save my life a short while back. That his Kevlar vest stopped it is neither here nor there as he couldn't be sure it would when his protective instincts kicked in.

The first task for today was to speak with the Berkowitzs. Howard had offered to let me name my price for finding the killer, I wasn't going to write my own cheque, of course, that would just be vulgar, but even if he had changed his mind now and no longer wished to hire my services, I was going to solve the case anyway because it is what I do.

We were heading to the hospital in Reykjavik first where Shandy was recovering still. A swift check of the ship's computer confirmed Howard had not returned to his suite, so I expected to find him there also.

We left via the private exit reserved for guests staying in the suites on the top two decks to find two of the cruise line's limousines waiting for us. They were sleek black cars, appointed with everything a person could think of. It was far too early in the morning to consider indulging in the fully supplied bar complete with icemaker though and we had all just eaten breakfast so we travelled mostly in silence, each keeping our own thoughts while the drivers took us through the city. The Landspitalinn National University Hospital was the largest in the area the driver, a local, informed us as we neared it. Unlike a taxi driver, who might be expected to babble, the driver only spoke twice during the entire trip and the other time was to greet us.

Lieutenant Baker already knew where to find Howard and Shandy Berkowitz which made the task of locating them in the huge building a simple one.

They were in a private room, which was to be expected of a billionaire and his wife, but they were not talking to each other and there was a sense of tension or of something unspoken when we joined them.

I went to Shandy's side, greeting her like an old friend even though we had only known each other a few days.

'Shandy, how are you feeling?' I enquired, giving her my concerned eyes.

She offered me a tight smile in return as the rest of my team filed into the room and spread out. 'I'm fine,' she assured me. 'The bullet didn't even touch me, the doctors said. Apparently, it got close enough to the skin to rupture it as it went by. I didn't know bullets could do that.'

I didn't either. 'Shandy I am here to find out who your stalker is and whether that is the same person who shot Grace last night.'

Shandy shot a look at Howard quickly before looking at me again. 'You really don't have to involve yourself, Patricia. There is no need. You are on vacation. Whoever it was will be long gone now.'

Howard interrupted her. 'They killed Grace, Shandy,' he stated bluntly. 'We've been through this, darling. The killer was probably aiming at you. I know that's a horrible thing to say, but why would anyone kill Grace?'

'Why would anyone want to kill Shandy?' I asked him, snapping out my question quickly since the topic was hot. I was looking at Howard when I asked it but focused on the woman in the bed again now. 'Why would you be targeted, Shandy?'

Howard answered. 'It's because of my success.'

'You don't know that,' Shandy argued.

My head was going back and forth like I was watching a tennis match, so I moved position to put them both at a better angle. 'What makes you think your success has caused someone to target Shandy?' I wanted Howard to clarify.

'I don't know,' he relented with a sigh. 'Shandy is right about that. It makes sense in my head that I would attract a few nutters. I made a lot of money and I suppose I expect that to come with negative connotations. I take it you know about the emails?' he asked.

'Yes. I need to see them.' Lieutenant Baker said he tried to get to see them last night, and Howard was evasive about them then.

Howard lowered his eyes to the floor. 'Okay.' It was clear from the tone of his voice that he didn't want to grant us access to the emails.

'What is it that is not being said?' I asked.

Howard's eyes twitched in Shandy's direction, a look of shame on his face.

Shandy explained, 'He had an affair.'

No one said anything for a few seconds. No one gasped or commented, the room was just silent until I asked, 'Is the person sending the emails attempting blackmail?' Was this why he was evasive about letting Lieutenant Baker see the emails?

'No, no, nothing like that,' replied Howard, his voice little more than a whisper as he continued to look at the floor. 'Whoever it is just wants to punish me.'

'I'm guessing the emails are not from the woman you were with?' I asked, making the assumption that it wasn't a homosexual affair.

He shook his head a little and brought his face up to look at mine. 'I don't think so. I made contact with her to be sure, but she is married with children of her own now and said she hadn't thought about me in years.'

'The affair was fifteen years ago,' Shandy explained, doing her best to keep the anger and emotion from her voice but mostly failing. 'I only found out about it recently when the emails started arriving. Howard and I have agreed to leave it in the past.'

'I need to see the emails. Can you send them to me now, please?' It was posed as a question, but my tone left little room for negotiation.

Howard nodded his head, a sad, small motion, and took out his phone. I recited my email address and soon I could hear the gentle chime from my phone as the messages began to arrive. I would send them to everyone on the team shortly and we would go through them on a bigger screen later.

Sticking with the theme of the emails, I said, 'We will have time to dissect the emails later. Before we do, please tell us the general theme of the threats.'

Howard glanced behind himself and, as if suddenly weary, he backed to a chair and sat himself in it. Yesterday, he had been larger than life and full of joy. Today he was withdrawn and hunched and spent most of his time looking down at the tile. I thought I would have to prompt him, but he started talking before I needed to.

'The threats don't make sense. That's the biggest takeaway.' I wasn't sure what he was trying to tell us, but I kept my mouth closed so he could explain. 'The stalker – I'll call him that so we have a name – claims that I am a thief and that I will get what is coming to me. The tone of the emails is generally the same: I'm going to make you pay for what you did, I will take everything from you, just as you took it all from me, just you wait, Howard Berkowitz, I'm going to kill you last, by which I assumed he meant he would kill everyone else I know first. I have no idea what it is that I am supposed to have stolen and I have no idea who the person could be.'

'You said, he, though,' Lieutenant Bhukari pointed out. Howard's eyes swung her way. 'When you referred to the stalker, you used a male pronoun each time.' He'd done it the previous evening too.

'It's just a guess,' he replied. 'I suppose it could be a woman, but I still have no idea who it could be.'

'How did the affair come out?' asked Agent Garrett, taking part in one of my investigations for once. More normally, he lingers in a corner, observing like a silent sentinel.

'That was in an email to me,' said Shandy, shifting the focus of the room. 'I told you yesterday that the emails have come from different addresses, so once again, we cannot be certain it is from the same person, but the tone and wording are very similar in all of them. I didn't know about the emails Howard was getting until I confronted him about the one I got. It all came out then but despite attempts to block them, they just keep coming.'

Lieutenant Baker had a question. 'Have you had anyone attempt to trace the IP address back to where the emails originated?'

I had wondered the same thing. I didn't know much about modern technology, but Barbie once explained how every computer has an Internet Protocol address which located the point where it connects to the network. It was something like that anyway and my shaky knowledge of the correct terminology was why I hadn't posed the question myself.

Howard fielded the question. 'I brought a team of expert hackers in. The messages were being rerouted all over the world to escape detection and when they finally traced them back to their origin, it turned out they were coming from an abandoned building in a small town in Oregon.' He locked eyes with me. 'I've never been to Oregon. I don't know anyone there and I certainly cannot come up with someone I have caused harm to who would then begin this quest for revenge.'

'How could they know about the affair?' I asked. I wanted to mentally label him as 'poor' Howard because he looked so bedraggled by the events around him: the threat to his wife, the murder of his sister-in-law, but he cheated on his wife and after my own husband did the same to me, I would struggle to think of Mr Berkowitz as anything more than pond scum.

Howard just shrugged. 'I haven't worked that part out either, but if you are going to ask if it could be her husband coming after me, she wasn't married at the time and it's not her father either because he is dead. Whoever the stalker is, I can shed no light on their identity.'

I let the information sink in for a few seconds. We had plenty of evidence to sift through now at least. It might not lead us anywhere, but it would keep us busy.

Lieutenant Bhukari pitched in with a pertinent question. 'When was the most recent email?'

Howard answered. 'Just over a week ago.'

'But you received a typed letter just yesterday, did you not?' I reminded him.

He hung his head again. 'I should have told someone,' he managed through fresh tears. His shoulders began to shake, and he looked up with a wretched face. 'Grace might still be alive if I had taken it more seriously.'

'You couldn't have known,' Shandy reassured him though I noted she didn't leave her bed to offer him comfort.

'It's my fault she's dead!' Howard wailed. 'I knew it meant he was on board. I knew he meant to harm those around me. Why didn't I tell someone?'

Sam, the kind soul that he is, went to the distressed man in his chair and tried to make him feel better by offering to get him a cup of tea. Howard snorted a laugh, but patted Sam on his shoulder. 'I think, perhaps I should get myself that tea.' He got to his feet, looking exhausted, and having not slept all night, he probably was. 'If you'll excuse me, I should like to get a little air,' he announced, heading for the door.

Pippin, Bhukari, and Agent Garrett had to step out of his way, but we let him leave so he could regain control of his emotions without a roomful of strangers staring at him.

I felt we had covered the subject of threatening emails for now. Reattuning my attention to Shandy, I shifted position so I stood near the foot of her bed and she could easily see me. 'Grace's phone hasn't been found, Shandy. It was in her hand right before the shooting, but it wasn't on her person or in her handbag afterwards and has not been found yet.' Shandy was showing me a confused face. 'Have you any idea what might have happened to it?'

'Her phone is missing?' Shandy questioned.

'So too her laptop,' I added.

'Her laptop,' Shandy repeated my words.

'In her suite is a charging cable but the laptop itself is missing. My conclusion is that both items contained information that would either identify the killer or cause embarrassment to someone if they were scrutinised. Who would want them, Shandy?'

She was looking straight at me and her pupils didn't shift when she answered, 'I have no idea.' Had they rolled up and left to engage the memory portion or up and right which they would if she were going to lie and needed to engage her imagination, I wouldn't have believed her answer. As it was, she convinced me that she didn't know.

'Was she in any trouble?' Lieutenant Baker asked, drawing Shandy's attention away from me to look his way. 'Financial? Problems with a relationship? Gambling or alcohol abuse?'

Shandy shook her head. 'If there was anything like that, she hid it from me.'

The phone and laptop had been taken and that was a clue, but I didn't know who had them or why and until we found the answers to those questions, the clue was a dead end. I changed tack and came at the identity of the killer from a different angle. 'You were standing right in front of the killer when he fired, Shandy. Did you get a good look at them? The muzzle flash should have illuminated the person's face.'

'Maybe it did,' she made a face which said I-don't-know-what-to-tell-you. 'I guess I blinked, or I was looking the other way. I didn't see anyone.'

Speaking to Lieutenant Baker, I asked, 'You brought the schematic along, yes?' I knew he had already, I was just prompting him to produce it. It had been created on a computer but was too small to see on the handheld PDAs the security team are issued so they had printed it onto an A1 sheet.

Baker nudged Pippin, who produced the rolled paper from behind his back. It was inside a tube to protect it but moments later was spread out on the bed in front of Mrs Berkowitz.

'This is a schematic of the ballroom with all the guests marked with their positions at the time of the shooting. We have done some of this using pictures taken moments before the lights went out and by somewhat painstakingly working out relative positions.' On the computer, each of the little circles displayed a name that would highlight when the mouse clicker was rolled over it. We couldn't do that on paper but that was kind of the point. 'Can you show me where you and Grace were standing, please?'

Shandy stared down at the sheet of paper, held on either side by Pippin and Sam to keep it from rolling up again. Hesitantly, she reached out with her right index finger. 'Right about here, I think.' She tapped a pair of circles. 'That would be me and that would be Grace. I was standing in front of Howard, and he was in the middle of the stage.' I was getting looks from Baker, Bhukari, and Garrett, none of whom could fathom where I was going with this. Truthfully, I didn't know why I was asking either. Something bothered me about no one seeing the killer, and the killer being able to see in the dark.

You might come up with an immediate answer to do with night vision goggles because you've seen them on TV or in a movie, but the lenses emit a glow and if it was there, someone should have seen it, most especially the woman who got shot.

Something wasn't adding up already, but that was completely normal. I just had to find out what it was that unbalanced the equation and then I would have the answer to the case. For now, I felt like we were done at the hospital.

'Have they indicated how soon you can leave?' I asked Shandy.

She sat forward so she could rearrange her pillows as Pippin wound the schematic back up and put it away. 'I can go whenever I wish. The plastic surgeon Howard brought in said there might be a scar, but it is too early to perform surgery to correct it yet. The wound is dressed and that is all they can do for now. I think we would both like to get home.'

It was time to head back to the ship; we had much work to do. I left Lieutenant Baker with her as he needed to discuss the fact that they were currently not allowed to leave the ship until the case had been investigated – it ought to take no more than a day or possibly two to conclude any elements for which we needed the Berkowitzs, but they had to remain close by until cleared to leave if that was their intention.

Pippin opened the door, letting Sam out first, but my plan of heading back to the ship to dig through the emails went immediately sideways at the sight in the corridor outside.

Chase

Coming to a halt ten yards in front of us was a man holding a bunch of flowers. He looked like a person in the hospital to visit a loved one, that was until he saw us coming out of Shandy's room and froze to the spot.

His reaction was instant, and it communicated shock mixed with panic. I think we all saw him at the same time, but Agent Garrett was the first to react.

A frown forming on his brow, Wayne shouted, 'Hey!' at the man.

It proved to be the catalyst that broke the spell for the man started moving fast. He dropped the flowers as he started going backwards, tossing the blooms into the air to create a distraction. Any question I had that he was up to no good was long gone by this point, but then I saw the gun he was using the flowers to conceal.

As he started to run, he fired two wild shots, both hitting the ceiling, and because his gun was already in his hand, he did so before any of us could even think of ducking. The loud reports from his weapon drove a spike of fear through me. I was reaching out to grab Sam at the same time, but he was throwing himself on top of Molly, trying to protect her with his body.

Agent Garrett, who had done the same thing to protect me the last time someone took a shot in my direction was more inclined to give chase this time. I was still on my way down to the shiny hospital tile when I saw his feet thunder by my face. He wasn't alone either as both Bhukari, and Pippin sprinted after the unknown gunman. Half a second later, Lieutenant Baker shot past too.

The man, whoever he was, had fired the two panicked shots, turned, and ran, vanishing from sight through a turn to his right three yards later.

It all happened in the space of about four seconds, so as Lieutenant Baker careened around the same turn to give chase, I was only just starting to get up from the floor.

'Mrs Fisher!' yelled Molly. 'Who was that?'

I had no idea, but I really wanted to find out. I came off the floor like a sprinter from the blocks, my arms beginning to pump as I drove upwards with my legs, then I trod on the trailing edge of my scarf which tightened around my neck and yanked my head back down as I tried to get up.

Usain Bolt I was not.

My forward motion carried me into a spasm-like stumble as my arms cartwheeled. I couldn't arrest my forward movement, I kept trying to yank the scarf up so I wouldn't tread on it again, but no matter what I did with my feet, I seemed to find the stupid, long woollen thing with every step, and eventually crashed into a water dispenser, knocking it over to send water glugging everywhere.

The everywhere the water went, included all over the floor on which I was now lying.

'Cor, that was spectacular,' observed Molly helpfully. She was standing over me, offering her hand to get me up. 'Are you all right?'

I didn't feel like complaining audibly about my soggy knickers, but the sound of another bullet being fired meant I didn't have to, and we were running again, the scarf abandoned behind me in the corridor.

Molly outpaced Sam and me easily, her youth and ballerina's proportions allowing her to achieve a far greater speed as she ran. The corridor we saw the gunman duck down was filled with terrified faces. Hospital staff were cowering in huddled pairs and trios, chattering about what might be happening in excited terms. Patients able to get out of their beds had come to the doors to look out. There was nothing to see now but ahead there was shouting and yet another shot was fired.

An expert in such things might be able to tell what type of weapon it was from the report, but my untrained ears didn't know if it was the gunman shooting, or hospital security. I knew the lieutenants and Agent Garrett had left their weapons on the ship, so it wasn't them shooting. The mantra reverberating inside my head was focused on a singular thought: don't let anyone I know get hurt.

Ahead of me, Molly burst through a set of double doors. They swung shut behind her, but as I chased as hard as I could, she suddenly vanished from sight. Two seconds later, I reached the doors and could see, even before I got through them, what had befallen my youngest charge.

She'd been tackled by security.

And now she was fighting them.

Two burly men were attempting to pin the young lady who couldn't weigh more than a quarter their combined weight. Before I could get to them, one of her feet lashed out, catching one of the blonde-haired men under his chin. It didn't have a lot of force behind it, but enough to shunt him backward.

The language coming from Molly's mouth was shocking. Not that I hadn't heard it before; she had treated my ears to one of her mouthfuls before when she felt threatened. Now wasn't the time to comment on it, and I honestly wanted to continue after the others chasing the gunman, but I couldn't leave Molly in case she actually did some harm and got herself arrested.

That went double when Sam threw himself into the mix. Just when I stopped running to shout her innocence, Sam ran by me to bodily tackle the man Molly had just kicked away.

'You've got the wrong people!' I shouted, though I was no longer sure who I was shouting at.

A door clanged open twenty yards to my right, more guards thundering through it as they ran in our direction. They were coming to give assistance to their colleagues who were getting the upper hand now against Sam and Molly.

'Hit him, Mrs Fisher!' yelled Molly from the floor as she struggled against the man trying to pin her in place. 'Kick him in the trousers!'

The chap was indeed correctly aligned for me to deliver such a blow if I chose to, but the hospital security chaps were just doing their job. They had the wrong people, but they didn't know that.

In a bid to defuse the situation before it got worse, I stepped in front of the oncoming reinforcements and raised both my hands. 'We are not armed,' I told them calmly. 'We were chasing the man who shot at us.'

I could see their pace slow as they looked at the middle-aged woman offering them no threat. They were right on top of us now and were treated to a fresh torrent of creative cursing from Molly and then a sharp outrushing of air from the man as she finally found her target.

She was beneath him still but shoved him off with her feet, and still lying on the floor out of breath from the effort, she punched a fist into the air in victory.

The fresh arrival of security guards mercifully didn't feel a need to tackle me to the floor, opting instead to surround me along with Sam and

Molly. They found their wounded colleague's plight quite entertaining and were making comments in their native tongue which I didn't need to understand in order to recognise the meaning.

'I think you should all come with me,' said a woman as she arrived behind the men. 'We have your friends in custody too.'

The Stalker

Sam had earned himself a fat lip during his scuffle with the guard he chose to tackle. It was bleeding very slightly but he wore the wound with pride as we were led through the hospital still surrounded on all sides by the on-site security team.

They were professionally polite – we gave them no reason not to be, well no further reason in Molly's case – but they were also unswerving in their demand that we comply with their instructions or they would use force. The local police had been called and we were to be turned over to them. They were escorting us to a secure area near the front of the hospital away from any patients or staff.

Already waiting for us there were Agent Garrett and my three friends from the ship's security team. They were all unharmed I saw instantly to my great relief. Like Molly, Sam, and me, they were not restrained, but unlike Molly and Sam they did not look like they had been involved in a wrestling match.

I looked around for the man we saw outside Shandy's room, catching Lieutenant Baker's eye. 'We lost him,' he admitted glumly.

That was bothersome.

'Please take a seat,' said the head of hospital security. Her name was Alita Thorndottir and she wasn't of a mind to believe anything we said. Her plan was only to hand us off to the police. The Lieutenants had all left their weapons behind on the ship as they have no right to carry them, nor authority as security officers once they are outside of the port. Agent Garrett hadn't brought his either, getting through immigration at the port would have been difficult with it. Had they been found with weapons, the rent-a-cop hospital guards might have taken a different stance with us.

I waved to Agent Garrett, 'Still alive,' I reassured him. He ran from me this time – chasing an armed man admittedly – but it wasn't I who lost him for once.

'You are all okay?' asked Deepa.

'The hospital security have been very polite,' I assured her.

Molly frowned. 'That one grabbed my boobs,' she complained while glaring at the man she kicked in the pants.

'I was attempting to restrain you,' he grunted, looking like he was still suffering the aftereffects of his injury.

I moved the conversation on quickly before Molly could take us down a new side track. 'Miss Thorndottir,' I called to get her attention. 'The man we were chasing was armed and he appeared to be on his way to harm Mrs Berkowitz. Do you have cameras fitted in the hospital that would have caught an image of his face?' I had memorised it but that wasn't something I could reliably use. I wanted the image run through facial recognition so we could identify him. 'He is probably the same person who shot at Mrs Berkowitz last night and killed her sister. He is therefore the prime suspect in a murder enquiry.'

I had her attention at least, her expression one of surprise.

'We already explained this,' complained Lieutenant Baker.

Miss Thorndottir frowned at the men in the room, which was when I noticed that she was the only woman among them. 'Why was I not informed? Who was it they were chasing and how did he get away?'

A tall man with broad shoulders and muscular arms looked down at her from his significantly more than six-foot height. 'We had no reason to believe they were chasing anyone. There was a report of shots fired and these people were caught running for the main entrance.'

'We were chasing the man who fired the shots,' said Wayne in a tone that made it sound like he had said it more than once already.

'You didn't think to check out their story?' Alita asked, her expression incredulous. 'Did you find the weapon?'

'They could have ditched it before we caught them,' the man replied, sounding sure of himself.

She switched to Icelandic to say whatever she said next. From the way she said it, I think it was the sort of language one should not say in church and it was aimed at all the men around her. Whatever it translated to, it got them moving and she swung her attention toward the seven of us sitting on a row of chairs against one wall.

'If what you say is true, then I will release you and handle the police myself. I sent six of them back to Mrs Berkowitz's room, that's where you said the incident took place?'

'Yes,' I confirmed.

'They will make sure she is safe,' Alita wanted us to know. 'She is the one who was shot on the cruise ship. I heard about that when I came in this morning. How are you involved, please?'

I cut my eyes to Lieutenant Baker. 'The three men in uniform are members of the ship's security team. It is their responsibility to investigate because the crime occurred onboard the ship.'

'This is an international waters thing then, huh?'

'Something like that,' I conceded.

'Can I ask who you are?' she directed the question at me alone. 'If they are involved because they are security, then are you their ... boss?'

'Their boss? No, I'm ...' I was going to say a detective, but it made it sound like the ship's security team were incompetent and needed my help.

Lieutenant Baker came to my rescue. 'Mrs Fisher is a special investigator assisting us with this case.'

His answer satisfied Miss Thorndottir and before she could ask anything else, one of the security guards reappeared from wherever she sent them with an embarrassed look. 'There was another man. We have a clear shot of him running into reception and out of it. You can even see the gun in his hand.'

Less than a minute later, we were all watching the footage. The scene started out showing people coming and going across the wide reception area of the hospital. Then, heads snapped around as a man sprinted into sight, weaving through the slow-moving pedestrians to get to the doors. We could indeed see a black handgun held in his right hand. A few seconds after that, the three white uniforms and Agent Garrett appeared from the same direction, but by then the security guards had reached the reception area and, seeing people running for the doors at speed, they moved to cut them off.

Pippin was in the lead and we got to see his moment of indecision as he chose whether to try to pile through the guards to continue the chase, or to obey their instructions. The hospital didn't issue the guards with sidearms, just stun guns by the look of it, but it was Baker's command that stopped Pippin. I saw his shout and Pippin turn to look as he slowed his run and accepted the chase was over.

'We have no authority or jurisdiction here,' Baker explained sadly. 'If I thought we might catch him, I might have tried to go through the guards despite the consequences, but the gunman was already out of sight and still armed where we are not. Chasing him had been foolhardy enough.'

'Who is he?' asked Miss Thorndottir.

Shell Casings

'So, who is he?' I asked Howard.

Our plan to return to the ship got changed the moment Alita had one of her guys find a shot where the man's face had been captured. It was on the way in, which took them a while to find because they had to go back through an hour of footage to find him arriving. They made a photograph by freezing the video feed, then sent it to Lieutenant Baker's PDA.

The PDA was now being shoved under Howard's nose.

'I don't know,' Howard stammered. 'I've never seen him before.' I was having trouble believing him, even though he sounded convincing.

I wanted to quiz Shandy separately, but she was bordering on catatonic, her eyes wild and focussed on nothing as she burbled over and over that she couldn't believe someone had come here to kill her. It was as if yesterday's event never happened.

'I can't believe it,' she said again. 'He was actually going to try to shoot me. Why would he do that?' Her questions were not posed to anyone, and no one answered. Howard held her hand and did his best to comfort her, but she looked and sounded like she needed a sedative.

Ignoring her, the rest of us were in a huddle.

'He took quite a risk coming here to finish the job,' Agent Garrett pointed out. 'Yesterday's shooting was planned. He had a device set up to kill the lights and a way to still be able to see his target, assuming that was Mrs Berkowitz.'

'I think we can be sure it was now,' said Lieutenant Bhukari.

The Reykjavik police were with us, doing what they needed to do because someone had fired a gun in a hospital in their city. That no one had been hurt was a miracle.

Reykjavik crime scene guys were working in the corridor outside of Mrs Berkowitz room. They had the ceiling panels out and were looking for the bullets. Two detectives were in the room with us, but they were already about done. The crime only involved the Berkowitzs and us in so much as the gunman was most likely here to kill Shandy and/or Howard. Since we were all planning to go back to the ship where the original shooting had taken place, and the ship would sail out to sea in a day or so, the detectives seemed content to leave it in our hands.

They were going to look for the gunman, circulating the picture hospital security gave them, but since we couldn't identify who it was, they had little interest in us. They took statements and left the room. They arrived back in the corridor just as one of the crime scene guys working there found one of the bullets.

'It was stuck in some expanding foam the original contractors must have used to fill a hole,' explained a man stepping down from a short stepladder. He had it between a pair of tweezers for all to see. 'It's perfectly preserved,' he announced in case anyone couldn't tell that by looking.

'What kind of bullet it is?' asked Sam.

'A point four oh,' said Wayne, showing off his knowledge.

'You have a good eye,' the crime scene man acknowledged.

Wayne gave him a lopsided look. 'Not really. I saw his gun. It was a Glock 22. They fire a point four oh round.'

I frowned. 'That's different from the murder weapon used yesterday.'

'He could have more than one gun,' suggested Pippin.

Lieutenant Baker pursed his lips. 'He could. It would be inefficient to have different guns that need different ammunition though. He had to go to the trouble of sneaking weapons on board the ship in the first place. Why complicate things?'

Lieutenant Baker wanted to get us moving. 'Mr and Mrs Berkowitz, are you ready to leave? I can have a limousine outside in five minutes and I would much rather you travelled with us escorting you.'

Before the detectives could walk away, Lieutenant Bhukari went after them. I could hear her asking for them to just hang around for a couple of minutes until we had the gunman's target safely away from the hospital. The police were armed, and the Aurelia's crew were not which would make a big difference if the killer were still in the area, watching and waiting for his next chance.

A little more than five minutes later, we were pulling away from the kerb inside a procession of Purple Star Cruise Line's black limos. Would we be safer on the ship? That was hard to tell. The ship didn't have the ability to do facial recognition software, and unless the chap was a wanted criminal or had a record, we were unlikely to find out who he was by approaching other agencies for help. Howard offered to throw money at the problem, his wife, Shandy, arguing with him about it as if money was something they needed to protect. I doubted money was the solution here though; I believed good old-fashioned detective work was required.

And that was going to start with us examining the stalker's emails.

Threatening Messages

We arrived back at the ship amid a flurry of snow which began falling only after we set off from the hospital. It was cold, which I'm sure comes as no surprise in a country called Iceland, but according to the driver, it was unseasonably warm and set to get a lot colder soon. I was glad for my hat and gloves.

Shandy and Howard were silent heading back onto the ship. Neither would look at the other though they were holding hands as we walked up the gangplank. At the door, Lieutenant Baker, who was leading the way, paused to speak with the two men positioned there to check passengers on and off the ship. He was making sure we could get inside quickly and easily, which of course we did. One of the guards had a message for me though.

'A message?' I queried.

'Yes, Mrs Fisher. From Dr Kim,' he replied. The guard was yet another member of the security team I recognised but hadn't actually met. I waited for him to deliver the message, an awkward silence ensuing when no one said anything for several seconds.

'The message?' I prompted.

'Oh, yes,' the man blushed. 'To call him when you are available.'

I tilted my head curiously, but before I could clarify that was the whole message, Shandy asked, 'He didn't say what it was about?'

The guard's eyes shifted slightly to the right to answer her. 'No, ma'am.'

Could it be something to do with the case? I wasn't going to find out until I made contact. I would call him shortly from my suite where I could ensure privacy.

Shandy had a concerned look and a deep frown but both evaporated when she saw me looking at her. 'I hope it's not bad news,' she said, suggesting that she thought the call might be about my health.

We travelled to the top deck in the elevators and left the Berkowitzs at their door as we carried onto mine. Finally back inside the warm comfort of my suite, we discovered the ever-wonderful Jermaine had prepared tea and a light luncheon of selected finger sandwiches and bite-sized cakes. It was all served on delicate platters for the team to help themselves.

When he was able to get me to one side, Jermaine quietly informed me that Dr Kim had called the suite looking for me less than an hour ago. The message had already been passed but his need to speak with me was so great that he had been pursuing me. I needed to call him right now.

Taking myself to my bedroom to do it, I used the ship's phone to call down to sickbay. The phone was answered instantly.

'Sickbay, Nurse Halloran.'

'Hello, this is Patricia Fisher in the Windsor Suite. Dr Kim has been attempting to get hold of me. Is he there?'

'He's with a patient,' Nurse Halloran replied. 'I expect he will be free shortly. Do you want to wait, or shall I have him call you back?'

'Please let him know I called and will be in my suite if he wishes to speak with me.'

'Very good, Mrs Fisher. I will pass that on.' The line went dead, leaving me holding the handset of the old-fashioned phone. I squinted at it for a few seconds, trying to guess what he might have wanted. Did he have a question for me? Or was he going to tell me something pertinent to the investigation? Convinced he would be calling back soon, I replaced the phone in its cradle, and rejoined the team.

They were camped out in my suite, a whole squad of us with Lieutenant Schneider, the big man of the team, back with us now after a few hours' sleep. Hats, jackets, gloves, and even several pairs of shoes were discarded as we made ourselves more comfortable. Sam got out his magnifying glass and used it to take a closer look at one of the photocopies we made of the printed message the Berkowitzs received the previous day.

The printed letter was another outlier - another thing that didn't fit. The stalker had sent them emails until now and each email had been cleverly routed all over the planet. Why type a message and print it now? Was it just to let them know he was here on the ship? If he planned to kill them, it could have sent them scurrying for cover.

Seeing me with one of the copies in my hand, Lieutenant Baker left what he was doing, and crossed the room to speak with me. 'Have you had a chance to inspect the original, Mrs Fisher? I think you will find it interesting.'

I held up the photocopy I held in my right hand. 'I am just about to read it.'

'Ah,' he gave me a knowing smile. 'The words will not give you the full story.' He was being cryptic, so I waited for him to explain. The original was in a protective plastic bag, which he opened because he wanted to show me something. 'It's the paper, Mrs Fisher.'

Now he really had me curious. 'What about the paper?'

'This is the fine-grain, high-quality paper the cruise line buys for the suites. It isn't available anywhere else on the ship, except maybe the captain's quarters. You see what this means?' he had me at a loss. 'The killer has to be staying in one of the ship's suites,' he concluded.

I thought about his statement and bit my lip. 'Is it not conceivable that someone could get hold of it even though they are staying elsewhere?'

He resealed the evidence bag. 'I guess,' he conceded reluctantly. 'It wouldn't be impossible, I suppose.' Looking a little crestfallen, as if I had just crushed his big clue, he started back across the room.

Calling after him, I said, 'You should check into it and see if anyone in the suites flags up as a potential suspect.' I got a nod from him.

Turning my attention back to the copy in my hands, I sat on the couch to read it, gaining two dachshunds about half a second after my bottom touched the cushion.

Do you think you can be rid of me? You took all that was mine and kept it as your own. You owe me for what you took! I know you won't pay though. To do so would be the decent thing and we both know you are not a decent man. You lie and you deceive, not just me, and not just people you pass in the street, but your wife too.

She knows now, of course, she knows what kind of man you are, and she chose to stay with you. That is her mistake. What happens now is on her head. She should have distanced herself.

Howard Berkowitz, supposeably the inventor of the algorithm that made him a billion, but nothing more than a con artist and silver-tongued charlatan. I am coming for you Howard, but before I get to you, first I will take away everything that you hold dear. Like me, you will be left with nothing. Only then, when you understand the misery you have caused, will I allow you to die.

An involuntary shudder passed through me, waking the dogs who looked up to show their displeasure. Anna made a grump noise and settled against my right hip again. The typed message read just like the emails. I had read them all now and the content was much the same in all of them – general threats to get even without giving anything specific about what Howard's crime might be or what getting even might mean. It sounded like the stalker intended to kill Howard and Shandy and everyone around them, but it only alluded to it. Whoever wrote the emails and the typed note was careful to never make their intentions clear.

Howard and Shandy had returned to their suite where they said they planned to stay. Shandy, more than Howard was keen to terminate their stay onboard and fly home. They could not at this time, but we were working hard to solve the crime and end our need for them to remain. If their safety was in doubt, we would have to let them go, but they were protected by two members of the ship's security team who were positioned outside their door, and a further two inside.

The stalker/killer would have his work cut out if he wanted to shoot Shandy now.

A knock at the door drew our attention. The dachshunds were a sudden barking blur as they shot across the carpet to see off the intruder.

Jermaine made his way across the room at his usual unhurried butler's pace, calmly clipping both dogs to their leads before opening the door. The caller turned out to be Verity with her little dog, Rufus. Instant excitement followed as the three dogs all battled to get to each other. Verity stumbled forward as Rufus leapt, and the dogs were soon a tangle of leads that could only be resolved by unclipping them.

'Mrs Tuppence,' Jermaine announced our guest.

Verity came out of the lobby area and into the suite's main living area with wide eyes. 'Goodness, it's a houseful.'

'Hello, Verity,' I called so she could find me among the crowd. 'We are just having some lunch if you would like to join us.'

She crossed the room, almost tripping on the dogs as they shot past her feet in an over-excited race to somewhere. 'What is everyone doing?' she asked.

Agent Garrett answered for me, which was not only strange but a little rude. 'Mrs Fisher is investigating the shooting last night. The killer tried to get to Mrs Berkowitz again at the hospital when we were there.'

Verity's eyes narrowed in a glare aimed at Agent Garrett and I thought for a moment she was going to berate him for being rude. She caught herself though and swung her attention back to me where she began looking up and down as if inspecting me for bullet holes. 'Was he successful this time?'

'No,' I shook my head, 'But I think that is only because we startled him as we were coming out of Shandy's room. She and Howard are safely back in their suite now with a detachment of guards; just in case.'

'Isn't this a bit too dangerous for you to be getting involved in?' she asked, sounding truly concerned. 'What if something were to happen to you?'

I waved my right arm around the room. 'I have a lot of protection, and I am not the target. I don't think there is any danger and I doubt the killer will strike again now. Our efforts are all about identifying who it is and catching them. We were able to get a picture of him from the hospital security cameras so that has been circulated to the onboard security. If he attempts to get back onto the Aurelia, he will be detained.'

'Is he a passenger?'

I looked at Lieutenant Baker for an answer. He said, 'That is yet to be confirmed Mrs Tuppence. It seems likely but the ship's central registry doesn't record faces and even if it did, we do not have the software for the computer to match the picture we have to one we might have from a passport and that would mean going through them one at a time. We could do that, but like I said, we don't record faces of passengers. There has never been a need.'

Deepa chipped in, 'It's likely someone from the crew will recognise him if he is a passenger. We have a team of our fellow security officers going around with copies of the picture right now.'

'We also made sure the police have the picture and asked them to make sure the airport authorities have it. If he tries to board a plane, he will get caught.'

Verity identified a flaw we had already considered. 'What if he got back to the ship before you were able to circulate the picture to the crew? He could be here right now. Patricia, I don't like that you are putting yourself in danger like this. You have to promise that you will stay away from the Berkowitzs in case the killer has another shot at them.'

I found my right eyebrow rising all by itself. Verity was imploring me like we were lovers or something and she couldn't bear the thought of me being in danger. I tried to stop myself from frowning but didn't do a very good job.

Verity looked upset but realised she had gone too far. 'Sorry, Patricia. I … I ah, I don't make many friends and I was hoping you and I would continue to meet for lunches and such when we return home to England. This business with a crazy armed killer has me a little rattled.'

As if by magic, Jermaine appeared with a cup of tea for Verity. In his hands, the delicate china cup and saucer looked tiny. Verity took it with a tight smile and a dip of her head in thanks. 'He's a treasure that one,' she observed as he returned to the kitchen.

I had to agree. 'I am not sure what might have become of me without him.' Truly, without Jermaine to set me back on my feet all those months ago when I arrived on the Aurelia, I might now be in jail having never solved the mystery of the missing sapphire.

'Then let us hope nothing happens to him either,' commented Verity ominously as she sipped her tea. It was an odd thing to say, and though it was nothing more than a poor choice of words, she made it sound like something happening to someone close to me was an eventuality I could not avoid.

'I just popped in to see if you were free for lunch,' Verity told me as she set her now empty cup back onto the saucer. She called for Rufus, looking about to see where the three dogs might have got to. 'I am clearly interrupting your investigations ...'

Worried that I might seem rude because I was itching to get back to what the team were doing and might be making her feel unwanted, I said, 'There's no need to rush off. You can join in if you want.'

She shook her head and called for her dog again. 'Where has that naughty boy got to?' she asked when he failed to respond for a second time. 'I really must get along,' she said in reply to my suggestion. 'There are things to which I must attend.'

I knew where Rufus was. He was in the same place as both of mine: begging in the kitchen to see if they could convince Jermaine to drop a morsel or two. I excused myself by saying, 'One moment.' Then wove my way through the people dotted about my suite to get to the kitchen counter. Sure enough, three hopeful dachshund faces were staring upwards. I scooped Rufus and carried him back to his owner. As I did so, I noticed something on his collar. Not wanting to draw attention to it, I shifted my finger slightly to make the thing easier to see.

The back of my skull itched instantly, and I had to focus hard to make my expression neutral. 'How is the training going?' I asked her.

She pulled a face. 'Terrible. He is such a pickle. He won't come back when I call him, he ignores me all the time.' She took him from me and cradled him under her chin. 'He's such a sweet widdle baba though,' she cooed at him. 'We'll get there on the training, I guess. I need to be more dedicated and determined probably.'

I offered no comment and let her go. Walking with her to the door where Jermaine already waited to see her out.

With Verity going out of the door, I could return to the task of examining the emails. I wasn't sure we were going to find anything, truth be told, and was hoping we would get lucky with one of the crew recognising his face. However, I now had something more pressing I wanted to deal with.

Checking quickly over my shoulder to see who was watching, I grabbed Jermaine's sleeve and yanked him out of the door with me. I had waited just long enough for Verity to get out of sight, but pulling Jermaine into the passageway with me, I knew I didn't have long to explain what I planned to do.

'Jermaine, sweetie, I need to vanish for a few minutes, and I need you to cover for me.'

Jermaine frowned. 'Madam, I will, of course, do exactly as you ask, yet I feel I must point out that Mrs Tuppence's concerns were not unfounded. There is a killer on board and the chance of the Godmother tracking you here must be given consideration. I will come with you, wherever it is you are going.'

I shook my head in an urgent manner. 'No. I have to be alone, sweetie. I promise I will explain why when the time is right.' My butler eyed me sceptically. I was going to run all the way down to Mike's cabin and prayed he was there though the chances were high he wouldn't be. He was on board to watch people who might be watching me, and he couldn't do that reading a novel in his room.

As luck would have it, I took too long organising my escape and the door opened to reveal a stern-looking Agent Garrett before I could get out of sight.

'Going somewhere, Mrs Fisher?' he asked. 'You wouldn't be trying to sneak off without me, would you?'

'Perish the thought,' I replied, trying to make my remark sound genuine. 'I was just ... um, I was ...'

Jermaine saved me. 'Mrs Fisher received a call from Dr Kim earlier and hoped I might know what it was about. She did not wish to discuss it in front of everyone else.'

Grasping Jermaine's lie, while also questioning why Dr Kim was yet to return my call, I said, 'Yes, um, it might be to do with some ... ladies' issues.' I made my face blush as I mentioned the delicate subject.

Agent Garrett took it in his stride. 'Regardless the subject matter, Mrs Fisher, you agreed to allow me to escort you wherever you need to go. Would you like to fetch your shoes?' he asked, glancing down at my feet.

He'd caught me in the lie, which really made my face flush with colour and heat. The ship was heated but it was cold outside, and the coolness transferred into some areas of the ship – no one would willingly go far barefoot. I was going to see the lie through now though. I couldn't hope to slip away to see Mike, but I did need to see Dr Kim.

Jermaine went around Agent Garrett to fetch my shoes but going back into the suite attracted Sam's attention. He came to the door just as Jermaine was coming back out. 'Everything all right, Mrs Fisher?'

'Yes, Sam. I just need to visit Dr Kim.'

He considered that statement for a moment. 'I think I should check in with mum and dad. Mum gets uppity if I don't let her know what I am doing.'

'Haven't you got your phone?' I asked him.

'I forgot to charge it,' he admitted with a grin, pulling the dead device from a trouser pocket. 'I tried to heat it with the power of the sun to see if that would put some energy in it, but it just melted a small hole.' He fished out his magnifying glass to demonstrate his science experiment.

I let my eyes flare and got why Melissa sometimes despaired of his antics.

'Shall we?' I asked Agent Garrett who was clearly ready and only waiting for me. 'We can drop Sam off on route.'

'You're coming too?' Wayne asked, noticing that Jermaine was still on the outside of the suite and the door was now closed.

'I have some dry cleaning to collect. The facility is close to the sick bay. I might as well attend to the task now and accompany you.'

No one saw any reason to argue, so we set off with a short list of tasks to perform.

We didn't even get to number one.

Attempted Murder

Making our way through the central hub of the ship, we reached a wide atrium like a shopping mall with shops, restaurants, arcades, and other leisure activities. It plunged several decks with a retractable glass roof above so the sun and warmth could delight when the ship was in warmer climates. Today, in Iceland, the roof was closed, and the space was artificially heated. It was still nice to walk through and I chose the escalators rather than the elevators for once.

I soon wished I hadn't when I spotted Mike and saw Jermaine's head and eyes whip around.

'Madam I believe I just saw ...'

'No, you didn't,' I replied swiftly to cut him off.

Jermaine persisted. 'It looked just like ...'

'No, it didn't,' I insisted, trying desperately to make him stop talking without tipping off Sam, who would shout and wave if he saw the detective from home, or Wayne, who I didn't want to know I had another mystery guest on board.

Jermaine closed his mouth while giving me a curious look. 'If you say so, madam. Clearly I was mistaken.'

The mall-like hub of the ship wasn't devoid of people, but there weren't anywhere near as many as one might expect to see if we were at sea. With the ship docked in Reykjavik, and our stay extended at the cruise line's expense, passengers had struck out to explore farther afield than they otherwise might. I heard one of the crew say less than half the cabins were occupied which was giving the crew an easy ride and bonus time ashore as they were required to put in fewer shifts.

Had there been more people around, I might not have seen Shandy walking toward us, but there she was, the stark white dressing on her neck making her easy to identify even at a distance. From her left hand dangled a bag from one of the restaurants – she'd gone out to fetch food.

My mouth felt like hanging open, I was that shocked, but changing my course to intercept her as she came past the fountain in the middle of the mall, she caught sight of me and waved enthusiastically.

'I felt so cooped up in the suite,' she laughed as we came near enough for conversation. 'I know that's silly, but I hadn't eaten much since yesterday lunch, food at the party never happened, and after Grace ...' her expression switched to tearful the instant she thought about her sister. 'Well, I just couldn't stomach any food.' She caught herself beginning to wallow and shook her head to clear it and rid herself of the tears. 'The guards weren't happy but ...'

I didn't get to hear what she said next because the seahorse squirting water just behind Shandy's head suddenly exploded.

Wayne shouted, 'Gun!' and leapt on me, bearing me to the deck whether I wanted to go there or not. I heard an ooooff noise as someone, a man, was struck by one of the bullets but all around us passengers were screaming and running, trying to get away.

Wayne wasn't taking any chances with me, grabbing me under my left arm to drag me around the base of the fountain and out of the shooter's line of sight. Protected by the marble, I felt safer, but my own security wasn't registering as my first concern.

'Sam! Jermaine!' I shouted their names, convinced one of them had been hit. Wayne was using his strength and weight to keep me in place while shouting instructions to someone. It sounded like he was trying to direct someone to where the shots had come from, but wedged under his chest, with my face pressed to the cool floor, I was having trouble making out what was being said.

I could hear Shandy screaming her fear, which told me she was most likely unharmed. It was the third attempt on her life in less than twenty-four hours if I chose to count the aborted attack at the hospital. Screaming for Wayne to get off me, I couldn't work out what I should pray for. Someone had been hit, I was sure of that, I'd heard the sound of the bullet striking flesh, but was it Jermaine or Sam?

Sam had only been shot a week ago and was still wearing a sling for his arm. Melissa and Paul had both discussed terminating their trip and had only stayed because I convinced them it would be more dangerous to return home. How would I look them in the eyes now if he were injured again?

The shouting continued, and Wayne continued to hold me in place. I knew he was doing it to protect me and possibly doing so at his own risk, but I wanted to get up and see for myself what was happening and what had happened.

The pressure came off me the next moment, Wayne swearing and cursing because the shooter had escaped again. I was far less concerned about the killer than I was to see who had been shot and I swear I didn't breathe or feel my heart beat as I scrambled back around the fountain to find out.

My hands went to my mouth as I saw the pool of blood Sam was sitting in. It wasn't his though, and it hadn't come from Shandy, my darling Jermaine had a hole through the top of his chest and was lying on his back, propped up on Sam's lap as he used his own white gloves to staunch the bleeding.

'Terribly sorry, madam,' he started to say, 'I appear to have ruined my uniform. I shall require a few moments before I can return to my duties. I do hope that will not cause any inconvenience.'

With my heart caught in my throat, a laugh still escaped me. I was trying not to cry as I knelt next to him and took over tending his wound. Two members of the security team came skidding to a halt next to us. One, a young Caribbean woman in her early twenties was chattering on the radio, coordinating more security to the area, and calling for medical assistance. The other, a young man, wanted to see how bad Jermaine's wound was.

'He missed and hit your butler!' cried Shandy. 'That bullet was meant for me! I can't believe this is happening. I really have a stalker and he is really here to kill me!' She was burbling again just like she had in the hospital, her words failing to make sense.

To my left, the female guard climbed into the fountain and started wading across it.

With the guard helping me, we carefully opened Jermaine's shirt. He was doing his best not to wince but there was a lot of blood coming from him and it would need to be replaced if he continued to leak at this rate.

'We have to get him to Dr Kim in sickbay,' I insisted to the guard. 'Right now.'

'It's really not that bad, madam,' Jermaine argued. 'It must have hit a vein but there's nothing vital for it to damage.'

He was right, the wound was a foot above his heart in the meat of his shoulder right at the top of his chest, but I argued anyway. 'It's a lot of blood, sweetie.' I looked around. 'Where are those medics?'

'I think I can stand, madam. Perhaps it would be wiser for me to make my way to sickbay rather than wait.'

'Don't you dare,' I growled as he tried to shift position so he could rise.

Shandy was still gibbering, the trauma and shock too much now. She had blood on her; not that it was hers, but her billionaire lifestyle had taken a wrong turn and she was unable to cope with it.

A door burst open to our right, white uniforms spilling out along with two medics carrying their bags of equipment and a portable stretcher they held between them. More white uniforms appeared on the escalator two decks above as forces converged on our location.

'You're going to be all right,' I told Jermaine, holding his hand tightly and hoping I wasn't lying.

A flurry of activity began as people started to reach us. The security team coordinated the search and the newcomers were shown where the shooter had been. It was background trivia right now, but I noted whoever it was had appeared at the edge of the upper deck where the open atrium reaches its highest point. It was right next to a door that led back into the accommodation areas. The killer could have popped out, taken their shot, and darted back in again.

'Found one,' announced the Caribbean woman, still sloshing about in the water of the fountain. She was completely soaked, the water spewing from the various holes still going because no one had thought to turn it off. Music was still playing too for that matter, the background noise one becomes accustomed to and ignores most of the time. It was playing away to itself now, utterly ignorant of the pain and anguish going on.

What the woman had found was a bullet. It was amazing that she had because the bottom of the fountain was covered in a rich coating of coins thrown in by thousands of passengers in hundreds of different denominations. She held it in the palm of her hand. I could see it was intact, but my attention was all on Jermaine. In the next second, the medic declared him stable enough to move and they were heading to sickbay right now and at speed.

Two of the guards were coming with us to clear the route but something was wrong.

'I can't raise Dr Kim in the sickbay,' one of the paramedics explained as he frowned.

Deep in my stomach, a small knot of worry formed.

Call the Doctor

In the ship's main sickbay, which was basically a small hospital where anything up to and including minor surgeries could be performed, we soon discovered why Dr Kim wasn't answering his phone or radio.

He was dead. So too his on-call nurse. Both had been shot at close range. The scene greeted us as we burst through the doors, both people lying dead just a few feet inside and next to the sickbay's reception desk.

For what must have been the third or fourth time today, my hands flew to my mouth as I stifled my natural urge to scream in shock. Beside me, Agent Garrett swore under his breath. I had known Dr Kim for months, meeting him not long after I first came on board. His murder was a terrible tragedy, so too that of his Nurse Halloran of course, a woman of about my age.

We all ground to a halt in the doorway, the scene stealing our breath and making us question what on Earth we were supposed to do next. The pause was only momentary though, the crew leaping back into action as the security guards both grabbed for their radios and the medics ran forward to check what they already knew to be true: there was nothing to be done for the killer's latest victims and Jermaine still needed urgent treatment.

'We still need a doctor for Jermaine,' I pointed out, thinking straight even though my brain felt overloaded. The bleeding from his wound had mostly stopped now, but the bullet was still inside, and he would need surgery. He might be transferred ashore to a hospital for that to happen but the fastest way to get him medical attention had been the Aurelia's own facility.

'Dr Davis is coming,' shouted one of the medics, a man in his mid-thirties with a ginger beard and a fast receding hairline. 'He was on cabin visits,' he added.

I knew there to be three full-time doctors on board the ship. Sometimes they had little to do, the amount of work less than enough to keep one of them busy, but they had to be ready to attend to a serious medical issue twenty-four hours a day and more than one could occur at any time. Heart attacks, strokes, broken bones, and other less vital maladies could strike and did. The population of passengers on board had an average age somewhere close to sixty-five - that high because there were many in their eighties, nineties, and even a few centenarians who came aboard. Cabin visits for elderly passengers were a daily occurrence.

The news that he was on board and on route was some relief but not enough. I wanted Jermaine to be treated, not just given blood, and the stack of questions regarding the his shooting had just quadrupled because there were two more dead bodies to deal with.

Worse yet, the sickbay was now a crime scene. We needed to use the facilities to help Jermaine, but at the same time, we needed to stay out of it to preserve any evidence there might be.

It was something the medics and security guards were arguing about already.

'How about one of the medic stations on the passenger decks?' One of the guards suggested.

No one answered because Jermaine chose that moment to go all floppy. The medic tending to him, tried to rouse him, but quickly concluded we were acting now or risking his life. They overruled the guards but did their best to tiptoe around the bodies and blood blocking our path into the main part of the sickbay.

While the paramedics transferred Jermaine to a proper bed and got him hooked up to a number of monitors and devices that would check and report on his vital signs, I took a step back. My mind was awash with questions. I had seen so much since the first shot was fired yesterday evening that I was having trouble sifting and sorting it in my head. How had the killer got back on board? How had he known where Shandy would be to be able to get into position? How had he managed to get the weapons on board? Best one yet, why on Earth had he killed Dr Kim and the nurse and what was it Dr Kim wanted to tell me?

Dr David Davis crashed through the sickbay doors, barging his way in only to see Dr Kim and the nurse, and come to a sudden halt.

They hadn't told him!

The colour drained from his face and he reached out a flailing hand to grab something for support. His hand missed and he pitched forward in a dead faint. The security guys ran to his aid as did one of the paramedics, who then asked if the bodies could be covered over.

By the time Dr Davis came around, Dr Kim and his nurse were visible only as lumps beneath sheets ripped from spare beds.

'I'm sorry,' said Dr Davis, staring agog at the covered bodies. 'Someone shot them. Why would someone shoot Dr Kim?' His face was still devoid of colour and he was in no state to be treating Jermaine. Despite that, with the third of the ship's doctors ashore on leave, he was all we had, and I needed him.

Grabbing his collars and blocking his view of his murdered colleagues with my own body, I got into his face. 'You have an injured man, Dr Davis. There will be time for mourning and questions later.'

He looked shocked at my hard expression for a moment but closed his half-open mouth and took a deep breath. 'I'm sorry. That was quite the shock.' Getting to his feet and turning toward Jermaine on his hospital bed, he said, 'I had wondered why Dr Kim hadn't called me himself for assistance. Do we know what happened?'

'Not yet,' I replied. There was no further time for words of explanation because the paramedics were urging Dr Davis to get involved and reeling off facts and figures about his vitals and the nature of the wound. He gave instructions with clarity and precision, making me feel marginally less terrified for my friend's life. Jermaine was still unconscious, but I thought that for the best.

I let the medical professionals busy themselves and stepped away a few paces.

At my side still, Sam asked, 'Is Jermaine going to be all right, Mrs Fisher?'

Thinking hard about his question, I found myself biting my lip. Since I could do nothing to help, I was letting my brain work through scenarios in my head. There was one scenario in particular which scared the pants off me. It involved the Godmother and if my imagined sequence of events was anywhere near right, I was in a lot more trouble than I thought. It made my skull itch in a way I didn't like because it usually meant I was right.

To answer Sam, who stood by my side and held my hand, I said, 'I don't know, Sam. I really don't know.'

In the next breath, three things happened. The sound of running feet in the passageway outside announced yet more people coming our way. It was testament to how twitchy the guards were that they both went for their sidearms. Mercifully, it was Alistair who came into view with half a dozen more of the ship's security team on his shoulders. Simultaneous with the captain arriving, Dr Davis announced he needed to arrange to transfer Jermaine to hospital. He declared his condition to be stable, but the bullet needed to be extracted and the hospitals on land had better facilities. Then the third thing, which was a radio transmission for the captain.

He had just entered the room and was looking forlornly at the two forms beneath the sheets. He already knew who they were, of course, that was why he was here in person, but the radio interrupted whatever he had been about to say.

Looking annoyed that he needed to answer the call, he nevertheless leaned his head down to where a radio was clipped to his lapel and pressed the transmit button. 'This is the captain.'

'Sir, this is Lieutenant Schneider. We have identified the gunman from the hospital. He is staying in a cabin on deck seven. Our plan is to enter by force in a bid to surprise him if he is there. We will need to clear the deck though. What are your orders?'

They had found him. I closed my eyes and sent a silent prayer that this might be over now. If we could make the arrest and eliminate any further danger, we could work out the why and how of his crimes with a less frantic pace. It would also give me a chance to focus on the other matters which required my attention, although Jermaine was very firmly at the top of my list now.

Alistair was caught in a moment of indecision. He had rushed down here to attend to the matter of his murdered crew and see the gravely wounded Jermaine, who Alistair would refer to as Special Rating Clarke. Now though, he needed to deal with another, arguably more pressing matter, that of catching the person responsible before they could do more harm.

I watched him twitch but the choice was obvious, and I slipped my hand from Sam's as I went to him. 'The living, Alistair. You can do nothing for Dr Kim. Focus on making sure his death is the last.'

He huffed a hard breath through his nose, twitching his lips as he most likely cursed the stars, but he knew I was right. Pressing the send button again, he said, 'Hold. I am on route, ETA five minutes. Cordon off access to the passageways near the cabin and begin quietly evacuating passengers from the area. Stay alert and make sure one member of each team has their sidearm drawn and ready. Do not move without me unless the suspect is sighted. I want him alive. Out.' He flicked his eyes to his entourage of guards and then toward the doors, telling them to go.

He had to go too but chose to use the few seconds it would take to call the elevator to say something to me. 'How is Jermaine?' he used my butler's first name for the first time ever.

I gulped against a throat already sore from crying and blinked back fresh tears. 'Not good.'

Alistair pulled me into a hug, and kissed my head, surprising me with his public display of affection since no one knew we were back together.

'Captain?' the call echoed in from the passageway leading to the elevator. His team were waiting for him.

I pushed him away and said, 'Go. I'll see you shortly.'

He grimaced his disappointment at having to leave me among the dead bodies but jogged out of the doors with a final nod in my direction.

'What now, Mrs Fisher?' asked Sam. Even his permanent grin was absent today.

Agent Garrett stepped in to ask a question before I could answer the first one. 'I do hope you are not proposing to leave the ship with Jermaine, Mrs Fisher.' I eyed him critically, encouraging him to say something more. 'The ship, or rather, your suite is a safe place from which I can defend you. As demonstrated clearly in the last ... heck, less than a day,' he calculated, 'you have been shot at or had bullets flying near you no less than three times. I'm good, Mrs Fisher, but no one is that good. I'm just letting you know that if you attempt to go ashore with Jermaine, I am going to try to stop you.'

A retort found its way to my lips. An angry one at that, but as my eyebrows pinched inward in preparation for giving the Scotland Yard detective a piece of my mind, I saw an alternative solution and it was all to do with the ugly scenario involving the Godmother.

I switched my gaze to look at Jermaine, focussing on him when I asked. 'Dr Davis, how soon will you be moving him, please?'

He didn't look up when he said, 'Right now. I'm just compiling some notes. There is an ambulance on its way right now and we need to hustle to meet them outside.'

'Will you be accompanying him?' I wanted to know.

He shook his head, finishing what he was doing with a flurry of his pen as he signed off the bottom of the chart and attached it to the bottom of the bed. The paramedics were already extending the wheels downward by pressing a button so the whole thing, together with attached monitors could be taken down to the ambulance where he would be transferred. 'No, Mrs Fisher,' replied Dr Davis. 'There is no need and I fear I may be required here to perform autopsies.'

I wanted to go with Jermaine, but I could do nothing for him, and the vague outline of a plan was beginning to itch away at the back of my skull. It came with a question about how smart and how devious the Godmother might be. I needed Jermaine to survive because without him, going on would feel empty. However, in his injury, there occurred an opportunity.

Looking back at Agent Garrett, I gave him a hard look that failed to intimidate him as I knew it wouldn't. 'I will stay on board, Agent Garrett. But I am going to deck seven. I want to see the conclusion to Grace Snoke's murder investigation.' I hadn't asked a question or made a suggestion. I was doing it and nothing short of him knocking me out and carrying my limp form back to my suite was going to stop me.

I waited for the paramedics to leave, getting them to pause just briefly so I could kiss Jermaine's forehead before they took him away. It left the two guards in the room to remain with the two bodies; a grim task if ever there was one.

I wanted a quick word with Dr Davis who was also remaining behind, and thankfully Agent Garrett chose to follow the bed and the paramedics outside into the passageway to wait for me.

What I said to Dr Davis shocked him deeply. I guess he had never been asked anything like that before in his career, but he said he would make some phone calls and see what could be done. I would have to lean on Alistair too, but as I left the bewildered doctor behind to deal with his dead colleagues, I felt the first small inkling of hope.

That is until I remembered I had yet to tell Barbie about her best friend.

Cabin Raid

It wasn't difficult to find the site of the killer's cabin; a huge area of deck seven had been cordoned off. They couldn't tell if he was inside his cabin or not, but they were going to proceed with caution and assume the man was armed and prepared to kill.

The cordon kept me away from the action so, like everyone else who had gathered, out of curiosity in their cases, I wasn't able to see anything worth seeing. We all heard it though as the quiet in the passageway was suddenly interrupted by a loud thump, which I took to be the door being breached, and loud shouts as the security team, undoubtedly armed and wearing all the protection they could get, burst into his cabin to arrest him.

When the shouting ceased less than two seconds later, I guessed that they found the cabin empty. Not that anyone came by to confirm my belief and most of the people who had been gathered around me wandered off. Nothing exciting was going to happen and whatever had happened hadn't been exciting either. When I spotted Lieutenant Schneider step into sight down the passageway, I called to get his attention.

Schneider didn't hear me, but an ear-splitting whistle made him look my way. Made to jump by the unexpected and loud noise, I jerked my head around to find Molly standing next to me.

She had two fingers in her mouth which was how she had made the high-pitched whistle noise. 'That got his attention, Mrs Fisher,' she grinned.

'How did you find me?' I asked after I checked to make sure Schneider was coming our way.

'Chance,' she replied. 'Pippin and the others all scarpered when someone finally identified the bloke who took a shot at us in the hospital.'

'Did you hear a name?' I asked as thus far I hadn't heard it.

She frowned, her eyebrows pinching together as she tried to remember. 'Chester something. I wasn't really listening; I was trying to work out why all the emails were filled with spelling mistakes, but the typed letter wasn't.'

Lieutenant Schneider called out as he got close enough to not need to shout. 'Mrs Fisher. The cabin is empty, but they checked the log and he doesn't appear to have come back on board since he left the ship yesterday. Do you want to come through?'

Schneider moved the barrier to one side to let me through - Sam, Molly, and the ever-present Agent Garrett following. Along the passageway and around the corner, we saw which cabin we wanted from the press of people outside it. Schneider had been stripping off his Kevlar vest and helmet as he walked, dangling them from one giant hand now, but other members of the security team still had their gear on. Alistair hadn't gone for half measures; I counted a dozen guards either wearing armour or in the process of taking it off.

The passageways on board the ship are narrow; about wide enough for a couple to walk along side by side. They were wider on the upper decks and in the leisure and entertainment areas, but down on deck seven, the very bottom of the ship as far as passenger accommodation went, they were tight, so passing between the people struggling out of Kevlar vests required turning sideways. Sam had gone ahead of me, weaving through the hole made by Schneider as he led us to the killer's cabin. I watched as he reached into his jacket and pulled out his magnifying glass with his one good hand.

I found Alistair already inside with Lieutenants Baker and Bhukari. There was room for me to join them but only just. Sam had paused at the door, wondering if he should go in. I put my hands on his shoulders. 'It's a bit tight, Sam. Maybe just wait here a minute while I talk to the captain,' I suggested.

I got the expected response. 'Okay, Mrs Fisher.'

Alistair's back was to the door until he heard Sam say my name. I was coming through the door when he turned around. 'Hello, Patricia.'

I touched his arm and stopped to look about. 'What have you found?' I didn't want to touch anything as I had no gloves on, in contrast to the people in the cabin who were already starting to dismantle it. Lieutenant Baker was carefully going through his drawers while Deepa Bhukari sat at the small desk with a laptop computer – presumably the killer's – open and being scrutinised.

Lieutenant Baker fielded my question. 'This is definitely the guy. We found a stash of point four oh bullets, no nine millimetre oddly, and nothing of a higher calibre.'

'Why is that important?' I asked.

'Because he used an assault rifle in the entertainment mall. The bullet that was retrieved from the fountain was a seven point six two millimetre round,' explained Deepa. 'A handgun wouldn't have the power or accuracy to hit anything at the range he shot from.'

From the doorway, Schneider said, 'How did he miss anyway? Less than one hundred yards to the target and he missed Mrs Berkowitz completely.'

Lieutenant Deepa Bhukari, a former sniper spun around on her chair. 'It's a fair question, but if he's not a shooter and handling an unfamiliar weapon for the first time. Then add in nerves and adrenalin. Could just be that he panicked. I'm more interested to find out how he got it onto the ship in the first place.'

Alistair huffed a breath out through his nose. 'That is a question which must be answered.' Now that I was looking his way, he drew my attention to the man's nightstand on which there were pictures of Howard Berkowitz. They had been cut from magazines or printed from pictures on the internet and each one of them had been disfigured. Not in an amusing way like a child might with a moustache, beard, and glasses, but with biro knives sticking from his skulls and fake blood drawn using a red pen. His eyes were gouged out in most of the pictures. There were also pictures of Shandy but on those all he had done to deface them was mark a large X over the face.

There really wasn't much question that we had the right man. 'Who is he?' I asked.

Alistair answered. 'Chester Ulmer. His ticket was a last-minute purchase and he joined the ship in Canada.'

'Any sign of Grace Snoke's laptop and phone?' I asked hopefully.

Lieutenant Baker answered. 'Not so far, Mrs Fisher, and we already did a thorough search. If he took them, he didn't hide them in his cabin.'

From the desk where she was sitting Deepa said, 'He was stalking them through social media. Mostly that was through Shandy as Howard's use of social media is all about his internet business and reading the impersonal nature of the posts, I would assume Mr Berkowitz has a person who writes them for him. Mrs Berkowitz however has been posting pictures of the cruise and talking to her friends about where she is and what she is doing. There was a lot of build up to the big anniversary party with most of her social media contacts flying out to Iceland to meet the couple.'

I asked, 'Does he comment at any point or give any indication that either of the Berkowitzs know him?'

Still facing the screen, she shook her head. 'Not so far. He appears as a friend on her feed, but I know I have people on mine who I don't know and cannot work out how they came to be there.'

'Me too,' echoed Molly from just outside the door.

I pursed my lips and frowned. 'Is he just a crazy person who took offense at how much money Howard made? Or is there a genuine reason for him to want to kill them? To stalk them and then track them to the ship with the intention of killing them – that requires a deep level of hatred. It has to have come from somewhere.'

Lieutenant Baker shrugged. 'I guess now that we know who he is, we can ask them.'

'We need to find him,' stated Alistair in a tone that suggested he wanted to wring the man's neck himself. 'I want to know why he killed two of my crew and shot a third.' As if remembering Jermaine suddenly, he asked, 'Any word on your butler yet?' Before I could answer, he said, 'Too early, I suppose. He will have only just got to hospital.'

I tilted my head and looked at Alistair properly for the first time since he left my room this morning. Moving into his personal space so I could whisper, I asked, 'When did you last sleep?'

He snorted a tired laugh. 'I'm not sure.'

'Shouldn't you recall Commander Ochi? You cannot keep going like this without burning yourself out.'

He sagged a little but caught himself and stood upright to his full height as if forcing himself to look and feel alert. 'We have identified the man now, so this is drawing to a close. If I recall my deputy, it will end his family time only for him to arrive back after this is all over. I can sleep soon. The big question to answer now is where is Chester Ulmer? According to the ship's passenger log, he isn't on board - I have people triple checking that now. Somehow, he returned to the ship without any of the guards realising it was him or getting his name registered on the system,' Alistair sounded angry about the security team's failure. 'Then he shot at Mrs Berkowitz with a high-powered rifle, hitting your butler, Jermaine Clarke in the process. How he got that on board is another question I want an answer to, and now I don't know where he is, so we are going to have to tear the ship apart looking for him.' He let go of a deep sigh. 'I will have to close all the exits again and post sentries outside to make sure he doesn't escape by going over the side.'

'Sir!' Deepa's hand shot into the air. The suddenness of her call got our attention, getting our feet moving to see what she was looking at on his computer.

'What have you got?' Alistair asked.

'I'm in his emails and a purchase confirmation just popped up. He just bought a plane ticket; Reykjavik to Portland, Oregon.' Looking over her shoulders, with more people from outside now crowding into the tiny cabin, we got to see her click the link. A fresh page loaded and there on the screen were the flight details. She swung her head to look at the captain. 'It boards in less than an hour.'

Alistair and I locked eyes, but it was Sam who voiced the obvious conclusion. 'He's going to try to escape!'

Alistair was on his lapel microphone instantly. 'To all crew aboard the Aurelia, this is the captain. Passenger Chester Ulmer, an American travelling alone, is on board and likely to attempt to flee the ship. He is armed and to be considered extremely dangerous. He has killed three people and is in possession of an assault rifle. His picture has been circulated. If you have not seen it, identify yourself to a member of the security team and memorise his face. Under no circumstances is anyone to approach or challenge him.' He let go of his send switch to speak with those of us in the cabin. 'I want to create a way for him to get off the ship. That's the only safe way to tackle this situation. Get him off the ship where he cannot endanger passengers and crew.' He pressed his send switch again. 'If you see Chester Ulmer, do not engage with him, but do report his whereabouts immediately using the ship's phone system. Until this situation is resolved, use of the ship's phones is for emergencies only. This is the captain. Out.' The second his finger left the transmit button, he swung his attention to Lieutenant Baker. 'Get that message out to all the areas and crew who do not have radio contact.'

Baker replied with a crisp. 'Yes, sir,' and left the cabin to get it done.

Alistair, tired and overworked, stressed and probably hungry, had displayed why he was the captain: clear headed thinking in a pressure situation to deliver easily followed instructions that would protect lives and minimise the threat. Now all we had to do was wait.

At least, that's what I thought we would do. Alistair had another idea though. 'I need access to the ship's tannoy,' he voiced his thoughts out loud. 'Where is the nearest access point, anyone?'

I looked about to see if anyone knew the answer. 'There's a service room at the next intersection but I don't know if that will have a link to the public address system, sir,' offered Schneider.

Alistair pursed his lips and nodded. 'Doubtful. I'm heading for the bridge. Continue working here. I want to know everything there is to know about Chester Ulmer.'

He got a chorus of, 'Yes, sirs,' from all the crew, and from Sam who echoed what everyone else was saying. However, when the captain left, making his way to the bridge, I went with him, my entourage tagging on behind.

'What if he already left the ship?' I asked, almost needing to jog to keep up with Alistair's determined pace.

I got a, 'Hmmm?' In reply. He hadn't realised I was behind him until I spoke. I heard him say something about the wasted hours his crew would spend searching the ship would be suffered gladly if no one else got hurt, but I wasn't really listening and he was leaving me behind as my feet began to slow.

What if he already left the ship? The question I posed to the captain echoed in my head and was replaced by another one: What if he was never on board? The ship's passenger logging system to monitor and manage people getting on and off might not be fool proof but the security guards Purple Star employed were high calibre – would they have failed to spot the man they all held a photograph of? Did Chester Ulmer have a secret way on and off the ship that no one could see him using? I doubted it, but what did that mean?

'Are you all right, Mrs Fisher?' asked Sam.

My forward motion had almost, but not quite, ceased and I was creating a log jam. Alistair had turned a corner and was out of sight. I wasn't going with him though; there was no need. I was going back to the suite where I was going to find out about Chester Ulmer, and I was going to quiz Howard and Shandy about it.

Nothing was adding up and it was time to find out why.

Someone is Lying

In the elevator on the way up to the top deck, Alistair's voice echoed out of the speaker inside the car. It shut off the music which until then had been playing *Lady in Red* by Chris de Burgh. The tune connected a memory of arriving on the ship and the state I had been in at that point. It was a time I would rather forget, even if it was the day I met Alistair and the day my entire life changed for the better.

'Attention all passengers and crew. This is your captain speaking. There is no need for alarm. However, there is a person on board who the security team are searching for, and this person may be dangerous. It is for that reason that the doors to the ship are currently out of bounds to all passengers and crew whether attempting to enter or exit the ship. This is a temporary restriction and will be lifted just as soon as possible. The following is a message for passenger Chester Ulmer. The doors to the ship are open. As you have just heard, all passengers returning to the ship have been held and no one will be approaching the exits which gives you a clear run passage off the ship. If that is not your intention, my officers will find you. I encourage you to leave and do so quickly before yet more security officers arrive. I am offering you safe passage from the ship at this time. My officers will not attempt to stop you. This is the captain.'

The speaker clicked and Chris de Burgh's dulcet tones returned.

'Do you think he will leave?' asked Molly.

Sam turned around to see what I might say but I didn't have an answer for her. Agent Garrett said, 'Probably not,' and that seemed to cover it. He would think it a trap, most likely. So if he were on board, he would be tucked up somewhere and the crew would have to find him. Personally, I was willing to bet he was on his way to the airport and I knew the team on board would have contacted the local police and probably the airport authority to alert them. He stood little chance of getting onto that flight.

From the elevator, we had to pass the door to the Berkowitzs suite, and I stopped to speak with the guards posted there. Offering them a smile, I said, 'Hi, guys. Have you just come on shift or have you been here a while?'

One, a South African was called George something, I thought, and it was he who answered my question. 'We are just about to be relieved, Mrs Fisher.' It helped that most of the crew recognised me; I had pseudo celebrity status on board due to some of the things that had happened, and that the captain was dating me last time I travelled.

I asked the question I really wanted an answer to. 'Sorry, is it George?'

That I knew his name drew a smile. 'Yes, Mrs Fisher. George Ebonyi.'

'George, did Mrs Berkowitz sneak out earlier?'

Their faces dropped and I knew why. She had lied about them letting her pop out. She'd given them the slip and had then been shot at and almost killed. They were going to catch hell from the captain later and they knew it. I felt a twinge of sympathy for them.

George didn't bother to hide his annoyance. 'She asked if we could help move a heavy trunk because they were going to start packing. It was in her bedroom and she wanted it on the bed. By the time we came back out, she was gone.'

I nodded. She had gone for lunch, but she didn't need to give the guards the slip to achieve that. 'Where was Mr Berkowitz at the time?'

George answered again, 'In the bathroom, Mrs Fisher. He came out while we were shifting the trunk and got the fright of his life. He said they wouldn't pack themselves anyway, they would have the butler in their suite do it.'

That made sense. I nodded and backed away a pace deep in thought. 'Thank you, chaps. Enjoy the rest of your day.' I left them with their monotonous duty and walked away. I could have knocked on the Berkowitzs door right there and then but chose instead to work out the connection between Chester Ulmer and his targets first so I could confront them with it.

At my door, I asked Molly, 'Can you see if Barbie is free, please? She'll be in the gym around the corner.'

Glad to have something to do, Molly darted away as the rest of us went inside.

Anna and Georgie rushed over to greet me, barking and wagging their tails playfully. In all the drama with Jermaine, it never once occurred to me that they were alone. The rest of the people in the suite had all vacated it and left the two tiny dogs behind. Not that they would have cared much: a dachshund is a creature more dedicated to sleep than any other I have ever heard of.

I wanted to call the hospital to get an update on Jermaine, but I knew it was still far too early to do so. I couldn't do anything much about locating Chester Ulmer either, but I could try to solve the mystery of why he targeted Shandy Berkowitz.

First though, I was going to have to break the news of Jermaine's injury to Barbie. It was a task I had put off for over an hour now, partly because I didn't want to do it at all, partly because I had hoped I would leave the sick bay with the certain news that he was going to be fine, but also because such news is best delivered in person. I wasn't sure how Barbie would take it and I wanted to be there to comfort her.

With a dachshund under each arm, I asked Sam to put the kettle on for tea and settled onto the couch to wait for my gym instructor friend to arrive. The thing I forgot to do was ask Molly to not break the news first, so when Barbie rushed into the suite a few seconds later, her face was pale, and tears were already brimming.

'Is he going to be okay?' she demanded instantly, pausing just inside the door as she wrestled with her emotions. We had run away to the ship, leaving behind her job and her boyfriend because of my involvement in the Godmother case. Now her best friend was hurt and though she wouldn't vocalise any blame on my part, she had to be thinking that none of this could have happened without me.

I left the dogs on the couch and met her halfway across the room. When I opened my arms, she fell into them and we hugged for over a minute, neither of us saying anything.

With her mouth next to my ear, she repeated the question, her voice nothing more than a whisper of air, 'Is he going to be okay?'

There was an answer I wanted to give her, and it pained me deeply that I couldn't. When the time came, I needed her to be able to react naturally. To provide a response, I said, 'I don't know, sweetie.'

Agent Garrett was in the kitchen making mugs of tea with Sam. It gave him something to do while the women cried. I had thought he was flirting with Jermaine a while ago, but I guess it came to nothing or they were very discrete, but he was unphased by my butler's injury. If it bothered him at all, he was doing a good job of not showing it.

Barbie pushed away from me, patting my shoulder as she stepped back and blew out a shuddering breath to steady herself. Her cheeks were streaked with tears, not that it affected her makeup because she rarely bothered to wear any – why cover flawless skin?

'What do we do now?' Barbie asked.

Sam approached with a steaming mug of tea for her; made just the way Barbie likes it. Molly was behind him with one for me and each had one of their own.

Molly said, 'Yeah, Mrs Fisher, what's next? They know who the killer is, and everyone is focussed on catching him. Is there anything left for us to do?'

I took a cautious sip of my tea, savouring the warmth. 'We still have no idea why he was stalking the Berkowitzs. I think they are hiding something. I thought it was just Howard, but Shandy felt a need to shake off her guards earlier. She snuck out to get food, but I think that was just a ruse to cover up what she really went out for.'

'Which was what?' asked Molly.

I flipped my eyebrows and started moving toward the desk and the computer there. 'That's what I intend to find out.' I gave Barbie an imploring look. 'Are you up for some research?'

Research

Doing research with Barbie felt very familiar. I wasn't able to count the number of times Barbie and I had crowded around the computer in the Windsor Suite to dig into someone's life. Today it felt like an odd thing to do which was all because Jermaine would normally be helping us or bustling around in the background fetching gin and tonics or preparing food. Also though, it felt strange because we already knew who the bad guy was and somewhere beyond the walls of the suite, a manhunt raged.

If Alistair hoped for a swift resolution to his problem, he didn't get it. At least, I assumed he didn't because there was no fresh announcement to tell the people on board the ship that the situation was resolved.

The hour Chester had to get to and board the flight he booked came and went. Was booking the flight a decoy to make his pursuers look the wrong way, or was he too petrified by fear to make his run from the ship? The Aurelia was an enormous vessel with more hiding places than could be searched in an hour. If he did the wise thing and stayed put, he eliminated the chance of being spotted and he might be able to stay undetected for days or weeks.

While elsewhere, the crew looked for the killer, we delved into what linked Chester to the billionaires next door. Barbie was all over his social media for a while, confirming what her good friend Deepa had told me about his online stalking. He commented on some of Shandy's posts which was how he knew they were going on the cruise, where they were going to be, and that it was their anniversary. His comments rarely extended beyond an emoji or a thumbs up and there was nothing malicious or concerning. The lack of his hatred displayed in his comments demonstrated a rational mind – anything else would have drawn attention his way and most likely have resulted in Shandy blocking him. I also knew he was intelligent, resourceful, and capable since he'd worked out how to sneak a weapon on board and plan a murder that he might have got away with if he hadn't missed and hit Grace instead.

His interaction with Shandy's social media feed was interesting but it shed no light on why he chose to target her or why he hated Howard. Whatever it was, it remained elusive and frustrating. Since Molly wished to help, she had been assisting Barbie and I had been working with Sam, keeping him entertained in many ways, but our search into Chester Ulmer failed to extend beyond basic background information. I didn't have access to the sort of software or search engines that could access financial records or delve deep enough into his life to find what linked him.

When the knock on my door came, I was all but ready to give up, my finger poised on the mouse clicker to look at a website landing page associated with his name.

Agent Garrett, the only one not involved in our research – it didn't pertain to his role on the ship – went to the door. I looked up when I heard a familiar voice exchanging words with Wayne in the doorway and got to see Alistair coming into the suite.

His hat was tucked under his arm and he looked yet more tired than he had a couple of hours ago when I last saw him. 'I've just come from next door,' he announced. 'I was able to inform the Berkowitzs that Chester Ulmer was shot and killed at Reykjavik airport in the last hour.' I couldn't hide my surprise at the news. 'Details are sketchy, and the report was at least third hand by the time I received it. However, it would appear that he was spotted and challenged. He ran and was fatally wounded.'

He was a killer, a stone-cold psychopath who chose to target a family because they were rich, and he was not. At least that was the only conclusion I could currently draw. Things still didn't add up though. 'How did he get off the ship?' I asked.

Alistair grimaced. 'I wish I knew. We have a big hole in our security measures somewhere. Or there was someone helping him. I'm embarrassed to say I don't know which it is. Either way, he got back on the ship and then got off again. He brought multiple weapons onto the ship and killed three people, wounding another. This is a major failing and Purple Star will need to hold an enquiry.' There was something he wasn't saying. I knew him well enough to recognise when he was harbouring a worry he wouldn't air.

'Can you rest now?' I asked, genuinely concerned that he was going to keep going until he collapsed.

Mercifully, I got a wry smile from him this time. 'Commander Ochi just returned. I haven't found out who sent him a message, but he was tipped off to the recent problems and cut his family time short.'

'That was good of him,' I said. Agent Garrett hadn't hung around to listen once he let the captain in. He was back in the kitchen, currently rooting through the refrigerator. Seeing him do so made me glance at my watch: the day had gone. I knew the sun had set but this far north it did that during the early afternoon. It was dinner time now and perhaps that gave me an excuse to stop for a while. In the last day, so much had happened I could barely list it all in my head, but right at the top needed to be the rekindling of my relationship with Alistair.

We spent the night together before he had to rush off to attend to his duties. There hadn't been time or opportunity for us to discuss what that might mean since. We were standing apart from the other people in the suite, but it was hardly the right space for an intimate discussion.

I reached out for his hand. 'I think Commander Ochi's return means you can get some sleep. Will you let me settle you in?' I asked with a sultry smile. I hoped that by enticing him back to his private quarters behind the bridge, I might get him into bed. My sole intention was for him to sleep. Anything else could come once he was rested.

He took my hand and met my smile with a wolfish one of his own: he wasn't feeling that tired then. 'I need to eat. Will you join me?'

'For dinner?' It hadn't occurred to me; I was so engrossed in the research part of the investigation, but I had to acknowledge that it was time to take a break, let my head stop spinning, and relax.

Still holding my hand, his smile softened. 'Yes, Patricia. If you can spare the time. I would love to have dinner with you. It has been too long.' I believed that he had questions for me, about my feelings and my plans for the future, but that he was holding off from asking them because he wanted to avoid applying pressure.

'Thank you, Alistair. I'm hungry now, if that is what you meant, but we can meet later if you need time to wrap things up.'

'Now would work just fine, Commander Ochi is already on the bridge. I'll call the chef and have him bring food to my cabin. Shall I order wine?'

Between one heartbeat and the next, I ran the potential of my evening through my head. I was dissatisfied with the outcome of the investigation, but the killer had been cornered and shot. All the evidence showed that the Berkowitzs had attracted a stalker. If there was a reason, nefarious and hidden by Howard or not, the fact remained that Chester Ulmer had targeted them, decided Shandy needed to die, and then accidentally killed her sister Grace in the process. I had a crime, and a criminal, and it was all very neat. There were holes in it still but no glaring red flags that demanded I continue pursuing the answers at the cost of everything else.

I could let it go and have a night off. If I did that everything would be just the same in the morning as it was now.

What about Jermaine though? 'I ought to visit Jermaine,' I told Alistair.

There might have been a flicker of disappointment in his eyes, but it was so fleeting – because he shot it down as fast as it rose – that I couldn't be sure I had seen it all.

He said, 'Of course.'

Barbie had other ideas. 'I will check on Jermaine. If he is out of surgery, he may or may not be talking. You should go with the dinner and wine option, Patty.'

Agent Garrett chipped in. 'I would much rather you stayed on board the ship, Mrs Fisher. Your ability to act as a bullet magnet is making my face twitch.'

Molly and Sam also voiced their opinions, the chorus of the room a resounding direction to abandon the triple murder case in favour of an evening that would be a little bit more all about me. I guess Molly and Sam both wanted to call it a day anyhow, and who could blame them?

I gave in and accepted my fate.

Looking up at Alistair once more, I let my smile reach my eyes. 'I believe you have a date for the evening, sir.'

Fit to Lead?

Alistair had venison steaks delivered to his room for our dinner. He served them with a bottle of Argentinian red wine that was like drinking velvet, it was so smooth. It was good enough that I chose to help him finish the bottle rather than having my usual after-dinner gin and tonic.

Once I could see the first glass ease some of the tension in his shoulders, I broached the subject of what might be bothering him.

'Security issues,' he reluctantly revealed. 'The latest one is going to be a problem for me.'

'How so,' I pressed him to explain.

'It follows on from other incidents and questions have been raised about my ability to captain this ship.'

His statement shocked me. 'Surely not.'

He shrugged. 'I cannot blame them for raising the question. We must all be accountable. I feel that there isn't anything I could have done differently. But in the last two weeks, the ship was almost sunk by Robert Schooner – several of my crew were killed during that encounter – then Chester Ulmer managed to sneak a small arsenal on board the ship. No matter whether a member of crew was complicit or merely incompetent, it is still my responsibility. That is the hat I agreed to wear. That he killed Dr Kim and Nurse Halloran is a tragedy heaped on top of another tragedy after he killed Grace Snoke. When the enquiry comes, it will be difficult for me to explain how he managed to get on and off the ship past my entire complement of security. Especially since they were alerted to look for him. Honestly, if they ask for my resignation, I don't see a way I could argue.'

For a very brief moment, I felt an upwelling of joy at the thought he might have to find work that wasn't on board the ship. He could come home with me to England and ... I stopped myself before I let the fantasy run away with itself. He was a ship's captain and he might never be content doing anything else. Was that the man I wanted? One day he might retire from this life and be ready to settle down, until then, I would be wrong to do anything but support him.

He fell asleep next to me not long after that, stretched out on the bed with my arms around him. He was dead tired, but though I also felt fatigued, I couldn't manage to find sleep as my brain continued to examine the quandary Alistair faced. How had Chester Ulmer snuck on and off the ship? It wasn't the only question bothering me, for there were plenty of holes in this mystery yet.

A message from Barbie pinged through to my phone. It was only mid evening, Alistair far too tired to stay up any later, yet Barbie had visited Jermaine at the hospital and reported back to me that he was alert and in good spirit. Tapping out my relief and thanks, being careful to not wake Alistair, I thought again about what his injury might mean and whether I could indeed be right in my suspicions regarding the Godmother. It was a terrifying scenario, but one that I suspected might come. If I was right, then there were already agents of the Godmother on board. Not just hired assassins this time, but someone more subtle and devious.

I guess sleep took me eventually but not until after I had whiled away a long time coming up with several more questions about Chester Ulmer and filling my head with nightmares about what the Godmother might have in store for me.

The next morning, Alistair and I took breakfast in his cabin. His private quarters are tastefully decorated and sufficiently roomy for a couple, or even a family, to live in long term. Sitting at the rear of the bridge, his dining area sports a floor to ceiling window looking out over the whole of the ship except the nose bit at the front. It was there that he asked if I was happy to be back with him.

He posed the question in a casual way, as if he were asking about my preference for luncheon, but it was a serious subject and a question that was not easy to answer.

I thought for a moment about what I wanted to say, sipping my tea while we looked into each other's eyes. 'Alistair, I find myself almost overwhelmed with happiness to be sharing my time with you again. Were you not the captain of a cruise liner, and were I not still married to someone else, things might not be so complicated. I think that perhaps, I love you.' It was the first time I had said it although he had chosen to say it to me many months ago. I saw his reaction in his eyes; relief mixed with excitement. 'I do not, however, know what that means for us.'

'It means we have something to work towards, Patricia.' He reached across the table to take my hand. 'I will not ask you to change your life, just as I am sure you will not ask me to change mine. I believe that is one of the reasons you left before: because you recognise that here on the Aurelia is my place. I believe you and I can find a compromise that will work for both of us if that is what we want.'

Our feelings for each other were out in the open. It was done. How we worked out the future to fit our individual and combined needs was now down to us. We talked for half an hour, meandering our way through breakfast as a steward brought plates and refilled cups.

Anna and Georgie watched the steward going back and forth with interest, but unlike me, who would habitually drop something that they would swoop upon, he didn't spill so much as a toast crumb.

Alistair needed to get to work soon, as did I, but as the steward cleared away the breakfast things, I asked him to deliver a note. He waited while I hastily scrawled my message and folded it to make a handmade envelope. Inside, I placed the keycard for my suite. His work in Alistair's cabin complete, he departed to deliver the note and I collected my things, ready to leave.

Alistair insisted he escort me back to my suite when it was time to go. He was wearing his full-dress white uniform and looked as incredible as ever. A decent night of sleep had rejuvenated him, and he had a spring in his step because I was on his arm. That he admitted as much put a spring in my step.

To appease Agent Garrett, or perhaps to stop him taking extreme measures, I called him from the captain's cabin to let him know I was on my way down. When the lift opened, Agent Garrett was there outside waiting for me.

'Good morning, Mrs Fisher,' he said with a dip of his head in my direction. 'Good morning, Captain.'

'Good morning, Wayne,' I replied. Alistair called him Agent Garrett, but it was then that I turned to him and placed a hand on his chest. 'Agent Garrett can take me the rest of the way from here. I'm not going back to my suite yet anyway.'

Wayne frowned. 'You're not?'

A Dog Called …

The door barked at me when I knocked on it. It wasn't the door barking, of course, it was the dog on the other side. Anna and Georgie both barked in response which in turn elicited more barks in a self-sustaining cycle that might never end if the dogs have their way.

Despite the noise, Verity looked surprised to see me at her door. She should have worked out the barking was going both ways because Rufus could smell my two dogs through the gap beneath the door.

'Oh, err, hello, Patricia. Is everything all right?' she asked as she came around the slim gap of the door to join me outside in the passageway. She had Rufus tucked under her arm to stop him escaping or being a problem when she opened the door. He was straining to get away now, wiggling his body and pushing with his feet because he wanted to see Anna and Georgie.

'Yes, thank you. I wondered if you might like to do some of that obedience training you mentioned.' My suggestion caught her off guard, and while she fumbled to find an answer I pressed on. 'I was reading online last night that dogs learn best when they copy what other dogs are doing. I give a command to Anna and she does it while sitting next to Rufus. Rufus will have a better idea of what is required of him.'

'Well, I guess I see what you are saying,' she cautiously replied.

'You were complaining only yesterday about how he doesn't come back when you call him. That is a basic safety behaviour right there,' I pointed out helpfully. Verity was dithering on her doorstep. On her feet were house slippers, but otherwise she was dressed and ready for the day. Even so, she looked as if she were trying to find an excuse to avoid the very training she herself proposed. 'I can take him right now if you like. I was just taking the girls for a walk.'

Verity glanced down at her dog and back up at me, her eyes betraying the reluctance she felt. 'Walter and I were just about to go for breakfast.'

It was a weak reason given in the hope that I might relent. 'That's perfect then.' My response was enthusiastic and complemented by me stepping forward with my arms up to take Rufus from her arms.

Catching her by surprise, Verity, clutched at her dog. 'Um, maybe ... maybe I could just delay breakfast for a while. Will this take long?'

I dropped my arms and gave her a big smile. 'You're going to come with me. That is even better. We can chat while we walk.'

She ducked back inside, then poked her head around the door frame again. 'I just need to let Walter know about the change of plans. Won't be a moment.'

The door closed, and I had a desperate urge to put my ear up to it. Wayne was standing silently just a few feet away though and listening at doors isn't ladylike behaviour anyway. I tugged the girls' leads slightly, taking them back a polite distance from the door to wait.

Just a little more than a minute later, the door reopened, Rufus rushing out though held in check by his lead. He was full of beans, excited to be going somewhere. I watched Agent Garrett, wondering if his face would give anything away. When I told him I was going to visit Verity, he didn't question me beyond showing his surprise that we were not returning to the suite. That might have been nothing more than an expectation that he was about to get breakfast, which I denied him. During the night, while running the nasty Godmother scenario through my head, I began to follow a line of thinking that suggested I was currently in no danger at all.

Staying with that idea, it was time to find something out.

As I set off walking, little Rufus eagerly pulling his lead to catch up with Anna and Georgie, Verity asked, 'Where are we going?'

'Ideally, we would take them outside where we had lots of space, but to be effective, we need to have distraction around us: smells, people, that sort of thing. I think opposite the food court in the mall is an ideal place for us to start Rufus's training.'

Verity shot her eyes at me, widening them. 'Isn't that where your man, Jermaine, was shot yesterday. I heard about that. Isn't it awful?'

I closed my eyes and thought hard about Jermaine and what I knew of his condition. A tear slipped from my right eye when I opened them and looked at Verity. 'We are British, Verity. We are supposed to prevail in the face of adversity.'

She absorbed that for a second before saying, 'Well said, Patricia. That's the spirit that got our boys out of Dunkirk.'

We walked in silence for a while, Verity giving me a little space. I hadn't wanted her to come with me, I'd wanted to get Rufus by myself, but I wasn't prepared to wait for that opportunity to present itself because I also had a bunch of other tasks pencilled in for the day.

From her cabin, we had to travel up to get to the mall in the middle of the ship. There, the enticing smells from the various eateries serving breakfast assailed our nostrils the moment the elevator doors opened. The dogs' noses were high in the air as they trotted forward. My girls were yet to have their breakfast kibble, but it was only just about time when they would usually eat. I hoped this wouldn't take too long, but they would have to wait either way.

About halfway to the food court, there were people milling around as they discussed what they wanted to eat, and others going back and forth having finished their meals or making their way directly to their chosen food destination. It would be an ideal environment for recall training if that were what we were actually here for. It wasn't, but neither Verity nor Agent Garrett needed to know that.

'This is perfect,' I announced loud enough for Verity to hear as I slowed to a stop. 'What we need to do now is split up. If you stay here, and Wayne goes over there.' I pointed to a spot about twenty yards away, 'then I need to go far enough away for them to all come to me.'

'What then?' Verity asked cautiously.

'I'll leave the dogs with you and when I get over there,' I pointed to where I planned to take myself, 'I'll call for them to come. Rufus only needs to know half a dozen commands: sit, down – which is almost the same thing with a dachshund – stay, come, heel, and wait.'

'Wait?' She questioned. 'What does wait mean?'

I handed her my leads and turned to Wayne. 'Wayne your job is to chase them or head them off if they decide to make a break for the breakfast tables. I don't think mine will, but you never know. Just be on the lookout for Rufus.'

He backed away to the rough place I had indicated. Whether he was needed or not was immaterial for the purpose of this exercise. Walking backward away from Verity and the dogs, I lifted my right hand with the palm facing outward, the sign I employed to teach my dogs to stay. Getting farther away, I answered Verity's question. 'Wait means exactly that. It's just a handy extra command that tells them to stop moving. It can be useful if they are off the lead and go near the road. When I signal, just let go of the leads.'

I stopped about twenty yards away and nodded that Verity should let the dogs go. Simultaneously, I called for them to 'come'. They all did, running to me excitedly, though it was Anna leading the way, Georgie following her mum and Rufus following them because the other two were running. I made a fuss of them all and turned them around.

'Now your turn,' I called to Verity. Agent Garrett was standing in an exaggerated relaxed pose with his arms folded. I suspected he was bored and wanted to get some food. The delicious scents of bacon and hollandaise, coffee and toast wouldn't help.

Verity indulged me, copying my actions and tone of voice when she called the dogs to her. We repeated it, the dogs shuttle-sprinting between the two of us with glee. When they got back to Verity this time, I backed up another ten yards; just far enough to ensure neither Verity nor Wayne would be able to hear me if I spoke at normal conversation volume.

Once in position, I called to Verity, having to raise my voice a little more this time to be heard over the hubbub of chatter from the restaurants a few yards away. 'This time I will hold my two here to see if he can come back to you by himself.' I heard her call out a reply as she let the dogs go.

Obediently, they ran to me. This was it then, the time to test a theory. The three miniature dachshunds whizzed across the floor, delighting and entertaining customers sitting at the outer edge of the restaurants. They are funny to watch, their tiny legs a blur as they achieved surprising speeds. Skidding to a stop, I patted each one again, making a special fuss of Rufus, and then hooked a finger through the girls' collars.

'Your turn now, little man,' I set Rufus facing the right way and gave Verity a thumbs up.

'Rufus, come!' she commanded. Her little dog took a stuttering step forward and stopped again, unsure what he was supposed to do without the other dogs running alongside him.

At a volume only he would hear, I said, 'Smoky, sit.' The little dog placed his back end on the deck without even looking around. The back of my skull itched. To follow it up, because one success does not a definitive result make, I tried, 'Smoky, down,' and watched as the little dog, more commonly known as Rufus, pushed out his front paws to place his chest on the cool marble floor.

I bit my lip.

Mike

After a few more trials with Verity and her dog 'Rufus', I declared it was enough for one session and asked Wayne if he had yet eaten. As I expected, his day had started too early to accommodate the most important meal. He played it down, but his belly was most likely rumbling. It provided a good excuse to call it quits.

I didn't ask Verity why the tag on her dog's collar bore a different name to the one she used. I had a good idea why already. Now I needed to prove it one way or the other.

'That was amazing!' she gushed when I walked back to where she was standing. 'I know he didn't come back to me by himself, but it really felt like progress. I shall write about this in my journal.' We'd discussed the ratty old leather-bound book she carried around more than once. It was permanently in her handbag, and always in the way of whatever she was trying to retrieve from its depths. When curiosity got the better of me, I asked her about it only to be regaled with a tale about keeping a journal.

I asked her why, to which she claimed she always had and found it soothing at the end of the day to record what she had filled the hours with.

I suggested to Verity we should meet again later this day if she was going to be around. That she wasn't going ashore to explore Reykjavik or the rest of Iceland, and hadn't done much exploring since we arrived, added to the sense of mystery around her. Why did she call her dog by a different name to the one he answered to? I could have challenged her directly on it, but something – maybe just my suspicious nature - told me not to.

Back at my suite, I had let the dogs scamper off to get water and filled their bowls with kibble. I knew from Agent Garrett that Barbie and Molly were both at the gym. According to him, Barbie suggested Molly might want to think about her fitness if she was planning to join the ship's security team. I wasn't aware they had fitness tests, but apparently they do.

I acted like I wasn't doing anything much until the moment Agent Garrett went into his room. Then I rushed to mine where I expected Mike to be hiding. The note and keycard I sent the steward off with were for Mike Atwell in cabin 34782. The note gave Mike instructions to observe the dog training from one of the higher mezzanine floors and to get back to my suite before me.

He started talking the moment he saw it was me. 'Okay, Patricia, I had a nice early start when the steward woke me with your note, and I thoroughly enjoyed the dog training display. Can you please tell me why I am now in your bedroom and why you sent me a keycard for your suite?'

'I think it might be Verity,' I stated simply.

'She checked out,' Mike replied with a frown. 'She's just a woman from the West Country. She doesn't have a job and her husband works on oil rigs so is away a lot.'

'I shook my head. Can you look into her again, please? Dig deeper this time. Use people you trust that are outside of the police if you are able.'

'What does Agent Garrett think?' Mike asked. 'He is with you the whole time. I watched you trying to train her dog and didn't see anything that would make me suspicious.'

'Agent Garrett is not to be involved in this,' I stated, making my tone as unswerving as I could. It caused Mike's eyebrows to show his surprise.

'Think about it. I wanted you here because I believe the Godmother would send someone she trusted this time. Hired assassins didn't work, even if they did turn my car and Angelica's house into Swiss cheese. After so many failures, she would send a loyal lieutenant instead. Based on that theory, you came along to watch the people watching me. Anyone who wanted to get close to me, such as Verity, was potentially an operative loyal to the Godmother. I would think it sounded paranoid if there hadn't already been so many attempts to kill me. The Godmother means to make sure this time.'

Mike frowned; he thought I was wholly wrong. 'But if Verity Tuppence is working for the Godmother, and here with instruction to kill you, why hasn't she done it already? She's had plenty of chances.'

That was one I couldn't answer, not with any degree of certainty. I worried that it tied in with the nasty scenario in my head which sooner or later I was going to have to voice to the team. To answer Mike, I said, 'I think that will become clear in time. Can you please dig into her past and see what you can find for me, Mike?'

He gave me a resigned shrug, his shoulders sagging in defeat because he knew he was going to do it. 'Fine, sure. I'll go all the way back to her childhood if you want.'

He was being flippant, so was caught out when I replied, 'That might be what it takes.' Now he looked exasperated. 'I think the Godmother has been undetected all this time because she is clever, and cautious, not to mention probably a little paranoid. I also expect she buys people in law enforcement around the world to make sure she stays one step ahead which is why Agent Garrett cannot know.'

Mike threw me a shocked face. 'You can't suspect him, Patricia. He took a bullet for you a week ago, and you said he chased another gunman when he threatened you yesterday.'

I nodded. 'Wayne Garrett is most likely a loyal and decent man, but what about his bosses? If I tell him what I suspect, if I were to ask him to do the searches I have asked you to perform, somewhere up the chain it would trigger a warning and the Godmother would know.'

His head bobbed in acknowledgement as he saw my point. 'Trust no one.'

He was almost right. 'Trust only those we are certain we can trust.'

I backed toward my bedroom door. 'I'll check the coast is clear before you leave. I don't want you accidentally running into Wayne on your way to the door.'

Wayne was sitting in the main living area. Squashed into one of the armchairs where he was watching the news. He had a mug of coffee on a table near his right elbow and a plate with a single slice of toast on it. Given the smear of butter on his chin and the crumbs on his tie, I estimated there had been more slices on the plate when he started.

Anna and Georgie were at his feet, staring up with a level of determined hope only a dog can muster. If they focussed any harder, the final slice of toast would levitate and make its way down to them. As I watched, he reached out with his right hand to snag the butter soaked, unctuous, morsel. Both dogs gave him a grumpy look.

I ducked back inside my room. 'Might as well make yourself comfortable, Agent Garrett is right outside. I'm going to make myself a mug of tea. If he moves, I sneak you out. If he doesn't, I come up with something and get rid of him.'

I passed Wayne, heading for the kitchen and doing my best to ignore the voice from my stomach that wanted thick sliced bread toasted and covered in lashings of butter. I'd been able to smell toast down in the food court, and now the scent permeated the air in my suite. Carbs for breakfast do not suit though if I haven't had a workout and I had eaten a light breakfast with Alistair already.

Pressing the kettle into work and taking milk from the fridge, I spotted Wayne down his coffee and get to his feet. This would be my chance to get Mike out of the suite. It wasn't though. Wayne chose to place his dirty mug and plate in the dishwasher before settling onto one of the barstools around the kitchen island.

He was playing with his phone, not really paying me any attention, but I could hardly sneak a man from my bedroom without him seeing it.

It was very different in the suite without Jermaine here. The whole feel of the place, the fact that I got to make a cup of tea for myself for once, all struck home.

As I fished the teabag from my mug, Wayne made an observation, 'I'm surprised you haven't tried to get out to see Jermaine, Mrs Fisher. I thought by now that you would be either haranguing me to agree to accompany you or you would have found a way to sneak out again. You had plenty of opportunity last night when you were out of my sight.'

I skewed my lips to one side as I thought about how to answer. In truth, I was desperate to see Jermaine, but Wayne didn't need to know that. The less he knew about Jermaine's condition the better.

I huffed out a dissatisfied breath. 'I do want to see him, but Barbie indicated he would be coming back here today. There seemed little point in going there in time to see him discharged.'

'Discharged already?' Wayne sounded surprised.

'Released into Dr Davis's care, to be more accurate. Looking at it that way, it's just a transfer between wards, but with the ship due to sail tomorrow, it's better to get him settled in back on board.'

Wayne accepted what I told him but had another question. 'What are your plans for the day, Mrs Fisher? I know I was trying to stop you going ashore yesterday, but here we are in Iceland. If you want to go somewhere specific, and you are content to go in one of the ship's limousines, I will be happy to accompany you. This is my first time in Iceland too.'

His question led me nicely to getting him out the way so Mike could finally vacate my bedroom. 'Actually, I wanted to see what Melissa might have planned for the day. She hasn't met Verity, but I wondered if us ladies – we are all roughly the same age – might head out for lunch somewhere.' Wayne lifted a single eyebrow. 'I think I will take a walk down there now and ask her in person. Are you ready to go?'

He clicked the button on his phone to lock the screen and swivelled his barstool through ninety degrees to get off. 'Are we taking the dogs?'

A New Day, A New Death

We were taking the dogs because I constantly worried they didn't get enough exercise or fresh air on board. They showed no sign that they were suffering but the cold outside made me reluctant to take them any distance with their tiny paws in the snow. I might have been worrying for nothing, but taking the dogs for another walk meant going back to my bedroom for my coat, hat, and gloves - no scarf this time. I wasn't really planning to go for lunch and would make that clear to Melissa. After a slow start to my day in which I had, in fact, been working on a separate case, that of the Godmother, I wanted to take another look at the Berkowitzs' investigation.

The things that failed to add up before, were still failing to add up now. Everything pointed toward Chester Ulmer as the killer. Everything. So why was it that I didn't trust the solution we had?

Mike agreed to give it a minute and to check both ways before he left the suite in case Molly or Barbie were on their way back or in case there was a member of the security team who might question who he was to be exiting my suite. I left him to get on with it, confident he could manage by himself.

It was a decent walk to get to the Chalks' suite even though it was only one deck down. I took the stairs, picking both dogs up to carry them under my arms to exit less than a hundred yards from their door.

Back on the deck, the girls dragged me onward, always eager to get somewhere. At the Chalks' suite I knocked and stood back a pace to wait for it to be answered. I hadn't checked to see if they were in, but it was still early to have gone out for the day and I was sure Sam would have checked in with me before going on a day trip.

I was thinking I might need to knock again when the door finally swung inward. It was Paul this time, but the smile and a good morning I expected didn't come. He looked glum. I was going to ask what could possibly have affected him so, but he swung the door a little wider which revealed Sam clinging to Melissa and crying.

I rushed inside, pausing only to ask Agent Garrett to wait outside; this was a private moment for the Chalks. 'What happened?' I begged Paul tell me, my voice respectfully quiet. Sam's head was buried in his mum's shoulder, his greater height and weight making it uncomfortable for her to hold him. She shot me the same sort of unhappy look I got from Paul.

'It's his friend, Gemima,' Paul told me.

'The girl with Downs?' I wanted to confirm.

He didn't confirm either way, but said, 'She fell down some stairs last night and broke her neck.' Paul was speaking at a whisper, but Sam heard him all the same, crying his anguish once more as the tears came with wracking sobs that shook his shoulders. Melissa was doing her best to soothe and comfort, but it wasn't going to do any good.

Paul turned away from his family to face me. 'He so rarely meets anyone with his same condition. They really hit it off. This has hit him hard.'

I found myself rooted to the spot, unable to determine what I could do or say and feeling certain there was nothing within my power. From my handbag came the trill sound of my phone ringing. It was Lieutenant Baker's name displayed on the screen.

Moving to the edge of the cabin, next to the door, I thumbed the button to answer it. 'Hello.'

'Mrs Fisher, good morning, this is Lieutenant Baker. I wanted to let you know the divers found a weapon last night.'

'A weapon?' I echoed.

'Yes. Beneath the ship. It was just as the message about Chester Ulmer was received. They were recalled, but on the way back, one of the divers spotted a handgun. It's a 9mm, Mrs Fisher. I'm on my way to see it now.'

'That might be the murder weapon used on Grace Snoke,' I murmured.

'Yes,' replied Lieutenant Baker. 'It might be. Apparently, the serial numbers are still on it. If we are very lucky, we may find it belonged to Chester Ulmer and we can close the lid on this case for good.'

I wondered about that.

'You have to go,' acknowledged Paul.

I nodded, feeling glum now. It was tragic that a young woman had died. I'd never even met her, but the impact it was having on Sam was hard to watch. Guiltily, I wanted to leave now and be able to distract myself with something else.

However, Sam chose that moment to peel himself away from his mother. His face was blotchy from crying, but he yanked a handkerchief from his trouser pocket proceeded to wipe his face. Then, with a loud trumpet from his nose, he declared. 'I have to go mother. Somewhere, there is a crime happening.'

It sounded like a line from a movie, though I couldn't say if it was or not. My natural instinct was to tell him to take the day off and give himself some time to mourn. Perhaps though, it would be better for him to distract himself.

'Are you sure, Sam?' I asked. 'You can sit this one out if you like.' I gave him the option and made it his decision: he wasn't a child, and too many people treated him as if he were.

He sniffed and looked at the carpet as his shoulders shuddered the way they do when someone has been really crying. 'Thank you, Mrs Fisher,' he said, still looking at the carpet. 'I think it would be better if I had something to do.' With that he straightened his tie and pulled the magnifying glass from his jacket pocket.

He was ready.

Setting off with my assistant by my side, and my Scotland Yard bodyguard a pace behind, I wasn't sure what to expect of the day. Whatever I might have expected, what I got, wasn't it.

A New Suspect

The security team have a base of operations to which they report when they start each shift. It is located in the bridge superstructure, but they have other outposts dotted about the ship and it was in one of those on the twelfth deck that we found Lieutenant Baker. He was with Lieutenant Schneider, the tall Austrian lifting his chin in a small gesture of greeting as we came in. He spotted Sam's still-blotchy face but was tactful enough to not ask about it.

Lieutenant Baker looked up when we were escorted inside. 'Oh, hi, Mrs Fisher. I thought you might like to know that we have already been able to trace the weapon to its registered owner.'

'That was fast,' observed Wayne.

Lieutenant Baker moved to one side to reveal the weapon. 'This is not your average, made by the million, handgun.'

Agent Garrett whistled appreciatively and leaned forward to inspect it. I had no idea what I was looking at but even my eyes could tell there was something different about it.

Agent Garrett continued to look impressed. 'I've never seen one of these. Not in the flesh, so to speak, anyway.'

'It's a first for us too,' replied Baker. Then he tapped the handgun with a pen. 'You can see that it has fired several shots since it was last cleaned, the carbon deposits give that away. However, it is mostly spotless, which suggests it was either cleaned meticulously by the owner or had never been fired before. My money is on the latter.'

They all knew something I didn't, and it was making my right eye twitch. 'Okay, gun nuts, what is it?' I demanded.

Agent Garrett pointed an accusing finger at the innocent looking handgun. 'That, Mrs Fisher, is a Bremer Invisible 9mm recoilless. It is made on a 3D printer from a specially hardened plastic and has no metal parts. It is undetectable by a metal detector, is outlawed in most countries, and costs more than I make in a year.'

That didn't put an accurate cost on it since I had no idea what Agent Garrett might earn, but it suggested that, so far as handguns went, it was rather pricy.

Lieutenant Baker nodded in acknowledgement of Wayne's claim and commented, 'I looked it up: they retail at forty thousand dollars.' That sounded stupidly expensive for a handgun. I believed something more vanilla retailed for a few hundred dollars, but as I thought that, Lieutenant Baker delivered the killer line, 'It will come as no surprise then to learn that it is registered to Howard Berkowitz.'

The casual name drop was like a slap to the face. 'It's his handgun,' I murmured, staring into space as my brain whirled.

'The uniqueness of the weapon is how we traced its ownership so quickly,' Baker revealed.

'That doesn't mean Howard Berkowitz pulled the trigger,' Wayne reminded everyone.

He was right, it didn't. 'It does beg the question about who threw it over the side though. Ballistics will be able to match the bullet taken from Grace Snoke to the weapon that fired it. If they are one and the same …'

Lieutenant Baker was a step ahead of me. 'I already stopped the team of stewards who were in the Berkowitzs suite helping them pack. We don't have to wait for a ballistics report to start asking questions. Chester Ulmer used a different round for the gun he fired in the hospital. I always thought it odd that he would use two weapons with different rounds. Dr Kim and Nurse Halloran were also killed with 9mm rounds. I'd be willing to bet my next paycheck they were all shot by the same gun and it is this one.'

'It's not that far-fetched for Ulmer to have more than one weapon,' argued Lieutenant Schneider. 'We've been questioning how he got them on board but maybe he didn't, and he obtained them once on board.'

Baker didn't like that. 'That's even worse from a security point of view. That would mean there is arms dealing going on that we don't know about.'

'Good point,' Schneider conceded. 'Either way, the question remains about who tossed the gun over the side? If Chester Ulmer was the one who fired it, how did he get his hands on it?

They were all good questions and we weren't going to get any answers standing around on the twelfth deck. We needed to visit Mr and Mrs Berkowitz because it was time for us to have an uncomfortable chat.

On the way back up, my dachshunds leading the party, I learned that Lieutenant Baker had already sent Lieutenants Bhukari and Pippin ahead of him. The four were yet to have their assignment to me rescinded, so Baker acted as he thought he should and carried on with the investigation when he heard about the gun. I wasn't the only one who saw flaws in the evidence against Ulmer.

Ticking away at the back of my head was a desire to find out how he got onto and off the ship without detection. With him being dead and all, the option to quiz him was denied me and though we had been operating under the belief that Chester Ulmer was the killer, the latest evidence threw that into question. That he was targeting Howard and Shandy Berkowitz was hard to argue; he had been stalking them for sure and turning up at the hospital with a gun in his hand left little question as to his intention. However, I spent a good portion of last night trying to work out how he got back on the ship after the hospital shooting, fired a gun which hit Jermaine, and then slipped off the ship again without detection. It led me to roleplay different scenarios in my head, many of which didn't involve him being on the ship at all. I asked a question, 'When they caught him at the airport, did he have the assault rifle with him?'

Baker and Schneider exchanged a glance.

'What?' I wanted to know what the look meant.

Baker's cheeks flushed slightly. 'I don't know, Mrs Fisher. It hadn't occurred to me to ask that.'

Schneider added, 'We found no evidence of a larger weapon in his cabin. It would be hard enough to get any weapon on board, let alone something the length of an average suitcase. I cannot imagine how he came to have it.'

Baker blew out a frustrated breath, then voiced the very thing bouncing around inside my skull, 'We can't work out how he got on and off the ship either, but he did. That he did so while carrying a weapon is even worse.'

No one could present an argument against that statement. The breach in security was a problem. If they knew of the enquiry Alistair felt certain would come, they showed no sign, but we were approaching the Berkowitzs' suite now and we could already hear the argument raging inside because the door was open. A hapless-looking steward stood in the passageway outside, glad to be out of the firing line.

As we neared the door, I heard a tirade of cursing from Shandy and was dismayed to find it was all aimed at Pippin and Bhukari.

'I'll buy the ship!' she threatened just as I came across the threshold. 'I'll buy the ship and have you all fired.'

'We don't have that much money,' Howard pointed out.

Shandy was well beyond listening to reason though. 'You think you have the right to stop me going home? My sister was murdered by a crazy stalker and you think you can prevent me from repatriating her body. It's a disgrace! I demand to see the captain. He will be the first one to lose his job over this debacle.' Lieutenant Bhukari tried to get a word in but Shandy shouted her down. 'You're the security on this ship? Well let me tell you, you are a joke! You come in here this morning stating that you have some new evidence that must be investigated before you can let us leave. Why aren't your efforts focussed on finding out how it is that the security is so lax that a maniac brought a gun onto the ship?'

'Yes,' I echoed her sentiment.

Shandy saw me when I entered her suite but hadn't paused in her rant to acknowledge me. Now that she thought I was jumping in on her side, she grasped it. 'Thank you, Patricia.'

Making a mean face, I stared hard at Lieutenants Baker and Schneider. 'Yes, security team. Explain how it is that Howard Berkowitz smuggled a gun onto the ship.' From the corner of my eye, I saw Shandy's victorious expression freeze and then shatter.

Baker and Schneider were not looking at me or attempting to reply to my question. They were watching Howard and Shandy to see how they would react. What I saw was genuine surprise from Shandy and desperate shame from Howard – the shame of someone who has just been caught.

Shandy's mouth hung open in mute shock. Casting her eyes across the room to her husband, she stammered, 'What ... what are they talking about, Howard?'

Howard walked a few paces to a couch and lowered himself into it. He wouldn't meet my eyes, or his wife's, or anyone else's for that matter. He kept them locked on the carpet. He tilted his head to one side, and I could see his lips moving. To me, it looked as though he were playing through different responses in his head, trying them on for size, if you like, to see which one sounded best.

When he still hadn't said anything for what had to be coming up on a minute, Shandy shouted at him, 'Howard!'

He twitched as if stung by an electrical shock, but even though he kept his eyes down, he started talking. 'It was the stalker, you see? I was a little rattled, so I bought myself a little protection.'

'One of the few handguns in the world that we wouldn't be able to detect,' pointed out Lieutenant Baker. He kept his voice even, but I noted he was holding his PDA out in front of his body and I was willing to bet he was recording everything that was being said.

Howard twitched his shoulders again in an almost nothing shrug. 'I figured there was no point bringing a gun to defend myself with if it was going to be confiscated the moment we arrived.'

'Why did you shoot your sister-in-law?' I asked, going for the direct approach.

Shandy gasped, her hands flying to her mouth as the shock hit her.

My question made Howard's head snap up finally, and it was horror that showed on his face when he looked my way. 'I didn't shoot Grace!'

he cried. Turning to look at his wife, he begged, 'You've got to believe me, Shandy.' Then he was on his feet and moving across the room.

The security team reacted instantly, all of them placing a hand on the butt of their handguns. No one drew their weapon, but the act of touching them encouraged compliance.

It was Schneider who spoke next. 'No sudden moves now, please, Mr Berkowitz.'

Lieutenant Baker added, 'We all just want to get to the truth of what happened.'

Howard, a billionaire sitting on top of the world, had been full of life and justified confidence just two days ago. Now he looked shrivelled and confused by his surroundings. 'I ... it went missing,' he stuttered.

'The gun went missing?' Lieutenant Bhukari sought clarity.

Howard nodded.

'When did it go missing?' asked Baker. Their hands had relaxed away from their holsters, but they were ready, and I prayed Howard wouldn't do anything foolish now that would get someone hurt.

He looked about as if trying to find someone among us who had kind eyes and might believe what he was saying. 'I don't know,' he admitted wretchedly. Seeing the looks of disbelief, he blurted, 'I didn't check it after I came on board. I knew bringing it was a stupid thing to do. I just ... I wanted to have a means to defend myself and my wife. Once I got here though, I found it in my luggage where I hid it and I almost threw it overboard.'

'Why didn't you?' asked Shandy, her expression and tone hard to read.

'It seemed wasteful,' he replied, shame making his face red. 'It's an expensive gun.'

'You're a billionaire,' Shandy snarled.

He snivelled shamefully in reply, 'Old habits, I guess.'

I was going to ask him about where he had hidden it and when he last saw it, but before I could, Shandy screamed and ran at him. 'You killed Grace!' she said a number of other things too, none of which were printable. There was too little time between her starting to charge, and her slamming into him, for anyone to be able to stop her. We were all facing Howard with us forming a rough semicircle around him. Sam was beside me taking it all in and Agent Garrett was five yards back by the door which he had closed once we were all inside.

All four members of the security team darted forward to stop Shandy but none of them could get to her before she barrelled into her husband. He made no attempt to get out of her way or even defend himself against her attack. As if he knew he deserved it, he waited for her to slam into him, but she hit with more force than he expected, shunting him backwards and thrust him away with her arms at the same time. He flew backward, arms cartwheeling as he lost balance and fell. Shandy followed through, snarling, swearing, and growling her anger as she threw herself bodily after him.

It was as clear a display of mindless violence as I have ever witnessed. Shandy, a mild-mannered woman from a small town in New Zealand was overcome by a rage that she couldn't control.

As if watching in slow motion, we all saw the terrible injury coming before Howard's skull hit the edge of the coffee table. It collided with a terrible crack, the downward motion of his body wrenching his neck to an angle that made me want to vomit.

He hit the carpet as a dead weight but Shandy either hadn't noticed or didn't care for she landed on top of him and started raining blows to his chest and face in a frenzied and uncontrolled attack.

She only got about a second to continue that abuse before Bhukari and Pippen, the two nearest Howard when she attacked, grabbed her arms, and began to haul her off. Shandy bucked and screamed and promised to kill him for what he had done. Baker and Schneider lent their help to restrain her and with all four of them tied up, it fell to me to check whether Howard was even still alive.

Howard Berkowitz was breathing, and he had a pulse, but he was out cold. I was kneeling on the carpet by his side, my two dachshunds, Anna and Georgie, whose leads I had thrust at Sam, were trying to get to me.

'Keep them there, please, Sam,' I instructed.

Three yards away, the lieutenants had wrestled Shandy under control and she was in a chair sobbing now as the onslaught of emotions caught up to her.

I caught Lieutenant Baker's eye. He rolled his and silently mouthed, 'Happy anniversary.' It was a moment of black humour in an otherwise humourless situation. Aloud he asked, 'How is Mr Berkowitz?'

I gave him my report, then said, 'We need to get Dr Davis up here. His neck could be broken, and I don't want to touch him or attempt to move him.'

Baker nodded. 'I saw his head hit the table.'

Pippin started talking the next second, his radio in his hand as he called for support.

Now that there was something resembling calm and Shandy couldn't hope to repeat her attack without going through Schneider – something your average wrestler would think twice about – I pushed off the carpet and asked her the million-dollar question. 'Shandy, why would Howard want to kill Grace?'

The woman who I had briefly thought of as a friend was curled into a ball on the chair the team had pushed her into. Her feet were tucked under her bottom and her arms were folded around her middle as if giving herself a hug. Her chin was on her chest as she sobbed, but I wasn't sure what she was sobbing about. Was it that she believed she lost her husband too because he was guilty of murder, or had this stirred up the grief about her sister again?

I had to repeat the question before she even acknowledged I had asked it. She didn't look up, but she said, 'I have no idea. They always got on so well. Who else could it have been though? He was the one standing on the stage that night. That's where the shots came from. He must have had the gun with him and when the lights went out, he saw his chance and shot her.' Then her head snapped up with a gasp. 'He was aiming at me!'

The entire investigation that had gone before was shifting beneath my feet. If Howard was Grace's killer, what was Chester Ulmer's involvement? Was he supposed to be the patsy? The question caught me like a right hook, and I ran back to check on Howard's condition again. I needed him to regain consciousness so he could answer some questions.

Shandy was hyperventilating, the sudden revelation too much for her to handle. 'He was aiming at me,' she gibbered, and in the next moment, I watched the colour drain from her face. She was either about to vomit or faint, neither of which was preferable. Thankfully, I wasn't the only one paying attention, Lieutenant Bhukari diving in to grab Shandy's upper half. With deft precision and a firm hand, she pulled the fading woman forward and shoved her head down until it was below her heart.

In the next moment, the sound of running feet could be heard in the passageway, Agent Garrett opening the door so the people approaching could come inside without having to knock. First through the door was Dr David Davis, his medical bag in hand, behind him were two medics to assist him and yet more security, one of whom was Lieutenant Kumar who I remembered from the party.

I stepped to the edge of the room to get out of the way – there was activity that required space – and also to give myself space to think. Chester and Howard: there had to be a connection, but what was it? The effort put into research yesterday evening proved that whatever link there might be, it was elusive or intangible, and we might never find it without Howard to give us a clue.

While the medical team went to work checking Howard and Shandy, I compiled a mental list of all the holes I could see in the mystery. It was longer than I cared to mention.

A brace went around Howard's neck to secure it in position. I wasn't really paying attention when they moved him onto the gurney and unfolded the wheels to pop him up to waist height for transport, I was too busy thinking about things like Grace's missing phone and laptop. They hadn't come to light in Chester's cabin so were still missing. Were we going to find them here?

'I don't think his neck is broken,' said Dr Davis once he levered himself off the deck. 'I will need to take him ashore. Since that option is open to us, it presents his best chance of recovery.'

'Is he likely to regain consciousness any time soon?' asked Lieutenant Baker, clearly keen to ask Howard a few questions.

Dr Davis looked like someone who was used to being asked questions he couldn't possibly hope to answer. He inclined his head toward the two medics in attendance. 'Take him to sick bay, the ambulance crew can collect him from there. Oh, that reminds me, Mrs Fisher, your butler, Jermaine Clarke, will be delivered back to us shortly. I thought you would like to know. He won't be able to return to active duties for at least a few weeks, longer if I get my way. I'll have to rely on you to keep him from doing things though, I know what he is like.' Lieutenant Baker was still waiting patiently for his question to be answered. Dr Davis dealt with it on his way to the door. 'Mr Berkowitz suffered a blow to the cranium, Lieutenant. The severity of such things is only possible to gauge with an MRI scan. I would hope that doesn't prove necessary because he regains consciousness first. Either way, I shall do my best to keep you informed of his condition. Good enough?'

'Thank you,' Baker replied with a dip of his head.

The medics had checked Shandy over and declared her condition to require nothing more than rest. We needed the suite though; there was evidence to gather, questions to ask, and electronic devices to inspect. Last night, the case had looked all but closed. Now it was wide open again and I had no idea what we were going to find next.

I saw Baker and Bhukari whispering to each other, discussing something in quiet. A quick glance brought Pippin closer to them and then he made his way around the suite and I realised what he was doing: looking for an unused room in which to stash Mrs Berkowitz. Like my suite, it had several bedrooms, Pippin picking the first one he came to.

Deepa Bhukari took it upon herself to deal with Shandy. 'Mrs Berkowitz, is there someone we can contact for you? Another relative perhaps, I know a lot of your family have been visiting with you?'

Shandy was fiddling with her sleeves, absentmindedly pulling them down to cover her hands. I doubted she was even aware that she was doing it. 'There's no one,' she murmured.

She needed comfort and there was no one else here that knew her. In two steps I was with Sam and taking the dog leads from him. I scooped Georgie, and took the unresisting bundle of warm, dopey dog to the person who currently needed her most.

Reaching Shandy, I unceremoniously plonked Georgie into her lap and knelt so my face was at the same level as the distraught, confused woman. Georgie tried to lick my nose. 'I once read that happiness is a warm puppy. I can't promise to make the sunshine roll in, Shandy, but I think you should come with me.' I stood up and stuck out my hand for her to take. She looked at it for a moment, but when I wiggled my fingers beckoningly, she took it. Shandy didn't make eye contact, but she hooked her spare hand under Georgie and hugged the little dog to her breast as she followed me across the suite and into one of the spare bedrooms.

I closed the door, shutting us both inside. I got about three paces before a gentle knocking started and Agent Garrett spoke through the door. 'Mrs Fisher, I prefer it when you stay in sight.'

I got a weary look from Shandy and I held up a finger to beg a moment of grace. At the door, I opened it a crack, just enough for Agent Garrett to see me, and I hissed at him. 'Go away, Robocop. It's just two ladies in here and two lady dogs. Nothing is going to happen to me in the next few minutes.' With a final angry glare, I closed the door in his face.

Shandy was already on the bed, cuddling Georgie who was rolling on her back and trying to bite Shandy's nose in a playful way.

'She is a sweet one,' Shandy commented. The dog had done what I hoped and taken her mind away from the situation she found herself in. 'I've never thought of myself as a dog person, but I could imagine having one of these in my life. She's adorable.'

'Try finding a puppy that isn't,' I replied. 'Dachshunds are pretty special though. They are just funny dogs with a whole heap of character.' I let Shandy play with Georgie for a while and then let Anna go, releasing her from my arms to join her daughter on the bed. She was jealous for the attention of a different person the way most dogs are.

For the next couple of minutes, we talked about the dogs, and I controlled the conversation so it wouldn't drift until I wanted it to. Only when I thought she might be ready did I broach the subject I needed to.

'Is there a reason Howard might want to kill Grace?' Shandy didn't take her eyes from Georgie but she did freeze for a second. Reluctantly, I pushed her. 'Could she have known something that he couldn't risk her sharing with you?' Shandy was very deliberately keeping her eyes on my puppy. I couldn't tell whether I had touched on something or not; she wasn't giving anything away. I pushed again. 'Could she have caught him having another affair?'

My final question hit the mark, Shandy finally flicking a glance my way and then back to the dog. 'I don't know,' she said quietly. 'She didn't say anything to me. I didn't suspect him, if that is what you are asking, but if he did kill her, I don't know why he did it.'

'Did you know Howard had a gun?'

She shook her head, rather than verbalise her answer, but after a few seconds added, 'I had no idea. I was never a fan of the American need to have guns in the house. He'd never shown any inclination to own one and I don't remember ever discussing it, but no, I didn't know he had bought one. He was right to hide the truth from me because I would have objected.'

I waited a few seconds to see if she would feel a need to keep talking to fill the space. When she didn't I pressed her again, 'A few minutes ago, you said Howard was shooting at you when he hit Grace,' I was sticking with the premise that he was the killer, 'What makes you think he would want you dead?'

Shandy put her head down to the two dogs on the bed with her and nuzzled them rather than answer me. When I persisted by asking the same question for a second time, she made excuses, 'I was just jumping to conclusions. I have no reason to believe he wanted to kill me, just as I have no reason why he would want Grace dead. We were happy. At least, I thought we were.'

I asked a few more questions but I was getting nowhere. Shandy genuinely didn't seem to know anything of use. She assured me Howard hadn't been acting strange or stressed – any more than usual, was what she said. She claimed, yet again, to have no idea who Chester Ulmer was, and said she didn't really pay much attention to what Howard did. They had so much money that it became a non-subject. She could buy whatever she wanted, and he wouldn't even notice. So long as she was happy and not moaning at him, he didn't much care what she got up to. It didn't sound all that much like a happy relationship, but I had heard of worse ones.

Leaving Shandy to rest, I brought the dogs out of her suite and put them back on their leads. 'I'm just going to put the dogs in my own suite,' I announced on my way to the door.

Agent Garrett was still lounging by the door, uninvolved in the search now being conducted by half a dozen members of the Aurelia's security team. Sam had chosen to join in, using his magnifying glass to scrutinise anything his eyes fell upon. They were all wearing gloves now, guarding against leaving any additional fingerprints as they continued to look for anything that might shed some light on the mystery surrounding this case.

I swept from the suite and back into the passageway outside. The suites were on the outer ring of the upper deck and the passageway outside the doors was floor to ceiling glass in places which provided a panoramic view of the world beyond. Some days when I left my suite, I saw the ocean outside. It might be grey, or azure blue depending where we were on the planet. Other times, there was a beach or a city outside and today that city was Reykjavik. I'd had opportunity to get out and explore the nation before all this drama and was beginning to wish I'd rekindled my relationship with Alistair a week ago. We could have been staying in a remote resort by a volcanic hot spring somewhere and missing all this horror.

Grace Snoke, Dr Kim, and Nurse Halloran were all dead. So too Chester Ulmer, killed by law enforcement as he attempted to flee the country. His name was still on my tongue when I swiped the entry pad with my keycard and pushed my way inside.

To my surprise, Barbie and Molly were inside. I said, 'Hi, ladies,' as I unclipped the girls' collars and let them go. They dashed off to see their human friends. 'Finished with your workout already?'

Barbie said, 'Hey, Patty. I have a class again in forty minutes, but Molly is finished exercising for now, aren't you Molly.'

Molly's skin was flushed red, but she looked fresh from the shower and was wearing day clothes: tight-fitting stretchy sports-brand leggings and a bright red hooded top with the Iceland flag on the back. It was zipped up to her neck and she had flipflops on her feet as she padded around the suite. 'I have a sore bum,' she told me, thinking it newsworthy.

Wayne snorted a small laugh at the teenager's choice of words.

'I had her doing squats,' Barbie admitted with a sly grin. I remembered my first ever session doing weights and things with the gym queen. Twenty-four hours afterward, I couldn't sit or walk, and I definitely couldn't go up or down stairs. 'Molly is really quite fit though,' Barbie acknowledged. 'The fitness test won't be a problem.'

'Thank you, Barbie,' Molly replied, then grimaced at me and poked at all her sore bits while looking at me with an aghast expression.

'I just popped in to drop off the dogs,' I told them.

Barbie looked up from retying her laces. 'Why? Where are you going?'

I quickly told them about the fresh development with the gun being found and what it might mean.

Barbie couldn't believe it. 'You think the man they killed at the airport might have been innocent all along?'

I scratched my head. 'I think innocent would be a stretch. He was here and we saw him with a gun in his hand heading for Shandy's room in the hospital,' I reminded her. By 'we' I meant Molly, Wayne, and me, not her as she was the one who had not been with us at the time. 'His cabin was filled with pictures and photographs of the Berkowitzs. That stuff could have been planted, I suppose, but my gut tells me he was genuinely stalking them with a view to killing them both. Was he the one who shot and killed Grace and then wounded Shandy? I thought he was, but I have to say I am no longer sure.'

Molly had a question. 'You still think he is connected to Mr Berkowitz somehow?'

I puffed out my cheeks and let the air ruffle my lips as it left my mouth – a sigh mixed with a frustrated I-don't-know. 'Choosing to come after the couple and going to the lengths he has to target them here on this ship takes a level of dedication. Would a person do that without deeply rooted hatred? Something in his past must have caused that.'

'Yeah, but we looked and didn't find anything,' Molly reminded the room.

I nodded my head. 'That's right, we didn't. I found something though,' a memory of the last thing I saw before I gave up last night surfaced. 'I found his name on a website.' Biting my lip, I crossed the room to the computer and clicked the mouse to bring it to life. 'Did anyone touch this since Alistair came to rescue me yesterday evening.'

Barbie said, 'I was using my laptop.'

Molly shook her head. 'I use my phone mostly.'

The screen blinked into life, and when I clicked the tab at the bottom to open the internet browser, the page I was last looking at sprang back to life. Barbie and Molly crowded around me. Even Agent Garrett moved closer so he could get a look at what we were seeing.

Barbie leaned over to take the mouse from me. 'This is just an old landing page,' she commented. 'How did you come to find it?'

'It was on the page of links that came up when I searched his name. 'It wasn't even on the first page. I guess I cannot be sure this is his website even because he can't be the only Chester Ulmer on the planet.'

'Probably not,' Barbie agreed. 'Whatever this website was for, there's nothing left but this echo of it. The site itself has been taken down.' She did something at the top of the screen that switched what we were looking at to give us a page of data. Now I was looking at numbers and letters, some of which was formed into words, but most of which was gibberish. 'This is the source HTML code,' Barbie explained, as if that helped at all.

Not wanting to put her off, but equally having no idea what she was doing, I said, 'Okay. What does that tell us?'

Her eyes were locked on the screen, flitting across the lines of code, and it took her a few seconds to get around to answering. 'Nothing yet. Can you give me a while?'

I sucked on my top lip, wondering what it was that she was hoping to produce, but said, 'Sure. Aren't you due back in the gym shortly?'

I got a nod this time, just as her hand lifted to trace along a particular line of code. 'Yes. Hopefully this won't take all that long, but if it does, one of the other guys can cover. It's just a bodypump class.' I'd once made the mistake of trying her bodypump class and managed to pass out halfway through, injuring a man in the process when I smacked him with the barbell I was holding.

I got out of her way as I wasn't adding any value and left her to it with Molly at the computer.

'Back to the suite next door?' asked Agent Garrett.

I passed him on my way out. 'Yes.'

Nail in the Coffin

By the time I returned to the suite next door, the security team, led by Lieutenant Baker, were well into their search of the place and they had already uncovered evidence in the form of nine-millimetre bullets.

'It's a spare clip,' Schneider told me, by which I assumed he meant an extra magazine. 'The gun might have cost a fortune but the rounds for it are two a penny. There's more,' he drew my attention to a clear plastic evidence bag lying on a table. In it was clothing; uppermost was what appeared to be a man's jacket. 'Pippin had the bright idea to check the Aurelia's laundry to see if they had any items on their way through the system.'

I glanced at Pippin, who grinned and did a double raise of his eyebrows to silently accept that he'd come up with a genius idea.

'It's a Brioni jacket,' Schneider revealed. 'It costs more than a car.'

'And it was stuffed into a sack along with underwear and other garments all bound for the wash,' added Pippin. 'It says dry-clean only on the label.'

I looked at both men, first Schneider and then Pippin. 'Come on, guys, spit it out.'

'The jacket tested positive for gunshot residue,' said Pippin with a broad grin.

'A lot of it?' I asked because if he was wearing it when he shot the gun, there would be more than a trace amount on the sleeve of the hand holding the gun.'

Pippin's smile fell away. 'No. Trace amounts, but he might have known to pull his sleeve up, or maybe he covered the cuff with something to stop the worst of it.'

As a single piece of evidence, it wasn't worth much. We all knew he was on the stage when the shots were fired. The witness statements all placed the muzzle flashes several yards away from where he was standing, but he could have covered the distance, taken the shots, and got back into position again. I ran it through my head, and while it felt improbable, it certainly wasn't impossible. That he owned the gun and had brought it with him was more damning, and all the factors were adding up. Just like with Chester Ulmer, the outstanding question to be answered, was why. Why had he pulled the trigger? Whether his target was Grace or Shandy was another great unsolved riddle. Maybe he was shooting to kill both women, but no matter what, I still couldn't make it fit in my head.

'Why do it in such a public way?' I asked out loud. Faces in the room swung to look at me. 'If Howard is the killer, why didn't he make sure he had an alibi? Why pull the trigger himself even?'

'He needed to be the one to kill his wife?' asked Lieutenant Pippin.

'He had an affair once before,' Lieutenant Bhukari reminded us. 'Maybe he was again and this time he chose to get her out of the way. A billionaire's divorce would be expensive.'

I was sure she was right but a shout from the bedroom ended our conversation. One of the other crew members involved in the search, Lieutenant Kumar, I discovered, had found a laptop and a phone.

'Aren't you still looking for Mrs Snoke's laptop and phone?' he asked.

'Where were they?' asked Baker.

Lieutenant Kumar indicated. 'Right where you see them. I haven't attempted to move them yet so we can record where they were found.' He got a murmur of support for doing the right thing, but we were crowding around the bed now. In the main bedroom, where most of the luggage was stacked, the suitcase with the laptop and phone was on the bed. In the process of working through all the luggage, Lieutenant Kumar had chanced upon the one containing the missing items.

'That's Grace's phone,' I claimed boldly. 'At least, it's the same cover on the phone.' I might not have been able to tell anyone what the cover on her phone looked like, but now I was seeing it again, I could picture it in her hand when I met her two days ago.

Baker stepped forward and picked it up. 'Might as well see if there is anything interesting that it can reveal.' He nodded his head at Pippin. 'Want to see if the laptop can show us anything?'

No one spoke as both items were powered into life. Thankfully, since we knew neither had been with their charging cables for two days, they still had enough juice in them to turn on.

Lieutenant Baker huffed his disappointment loudly. 'This has been wiped.'

Pippin swung his head around from his position kneeling next to the bed. 'Same here. It's been taken back to factory settings. Someone with more skill might be able to recover some files, but it looks pretty well wiped to me.'

'The sort of thing a person with a background in computers and information technology could do,' I pointed out and we all knew I was talking about Howard. The internet being what it is, instructions to perform such a task would be available to read and follow for a person with only limited skill. Nevertheless, Grace Snoke's missing laptop and phone were in a suitcase filled with Howard Berkowitz's clothing and the evidence was really beginning to stack up against him.

Lieutenant Baker was shaking his head angrily and thumping the palm of his right hand into his forehead. 'Arrggh! He went missing.' It was a cryptic statement that required explanation. 'Mr Berkowitz,' he provided. 'When Dr Kim and the medics took Mrs Berkowitz down to the sickbay, Howard vanished. Don't you remember? When I went down there to speak with them, he wasn't there and appeared a few moments later with an excuse about needing to fetch medication. I didn't challenge it – I saw no reason to. He could have snagged Miss Snoke's phone when he was next to her body in the ballroom and then gone to her suite to get her laptop while his wife was being treated.'

'He really did it, didn't he?' Shandy's quiet voice from the doorway behind us made us all jump even though it was softly spoken. My heart pounded out a few staccato beats as it fought to get back to its usual rhythm.

No one replied and certainly no one was going to confirm or deny her statement. She reached up to touch her neck. 'Was he trying to kill me and hit Grace by accident? Or was it the other way around?'

I had to feel for her. Less than forty-eight hours ago she had been on top of the world and celebrating her wedding anniversary. Now her sister was dead, and her husband looked likely to be the killer.

Her eyes were locked on nothing, staring into space as she talked. 'I thought it was over when they caught the stalker. You said he was heading for the airport, that's why I snuck out. I was going stir crazy inside the suite and we were being watched by the guards even though they were doing their best to be invisible. Do you think it was Howard who shot at me in the mall?'

The question caused a familiar itching sensation at the back of my skull. 'Any sign of other weapons?' I asked the room. It was an agreed fact that the shooter had used a rifle of some kind. In fact, the only conjecture on the matter was how they could have possibly missed their target.

'Nothing so far,' said Lieutenant Schneider. 'We'll have to thoroughly search everything to be sure.'

I didn't think they were going to find it anywhere in the Berkowitzs' suite. It was a scenario that terrified me, but one that also filled me with hope because of what it meant if I was right.

Shandy broke the silence again. 'Will I be allowed to go home now? I don't think I can stomach staying here any longer. If you need to continue going through my luggage, you can just keep it. All I need is a change of underwear and my passport.'

She looked utterly miserable, but she was holding it together. I understood her desire to be away from the Aurelia and all the memories it must contain, but Howard wasn't convicted yet. 'Shandy don't you want to wait until Howard regains consciousness? He might be innocent.'

She pulled a face at me. 'Come on, Patricia. If he's innocent, why does he have my sister's phone and laptop? Why did he bring the murder weapon with him? I don't know why he did it, but I hope they lock him away for ever.' She locked eyes with Lieutenant Baker. 'Am I allowed to leave my suite?'

He drew in a breath as he considered her question. 'Mrs Berkowitz you are not under suspicion of any crime at this time. I must ask that you do not leave the ship, but if you wish to leave your cabin, I will not stop you. Is there somewhere you wish to go? I can escort you.'

I suspected Baker's offer was born of a concern that she might commit suicide or attempt to harm herself. She gave us all a lopsided grin as she backed toward her own bedroom door. 'I'm going to the bar. If anyone wants to join me, I'm buying. After all, misery loves company.'

Lieutenant Bhukari shot her eyes at her other half, Lieutenant Baker, but I said, 'Let her go. I will join her in a little while and make sure she doesn't overdo it.' We heard the main suite door open and close, but then footsteps coming our way again.

'I guess she forgot something,' I murmured as I turned to face the door. However, it wasn't Shandy returning, it was Barbie arriving.

She had wide eyes and 'brace yourself' look to her face. 'Guys, you are never going to believe what I discovered.'

A Reason to Hate

Barbie had her laptop under her arm, but it wasn't folded shut; it was open and ready for her to show us her discovery.

'I know why Chester Ulmer wanted to kill Howard and Shandy,' she stated boldly.

We all stared at her in disbelief for a beat until I said, 'Okay, genius. How?'

She placed the laptop on the bed so both her hands were free to gesticulate as she began to explain. I glanced at the screen, I wasn't the only one, I noticed, but it still showed the same lines of code we had been looking at on the computer in my suite.

'Most people don't know this,' Barbie began telling her audience. 'But buried inside the code for each website are header codes which show where the code was created. Each country has a unique identifier, much like an international dialling code but then they have regional ones as well. We thought Chester Ulmer was from Oregon, but he isn't.'

'We checked him out,' argued Lieutenant Schneider. 'His home address is listed there. When the manhunt here started, police in the US went to his house. I read the report.'

Barbie nodded. 'That's right. He was living in Oregon, but that's not where he is from. He started life in Ohio.'

I closed my eyes the second she started to say it because right there was the connection. 'Where Howard is from,' I reminded everyone with a sigh because I had missed it. To be fair, there just hadn't been time to dig deep enough into every possible connection and Howard continued to deny he'd ever heard of the man.

Barbie didn't let my interruption stop her. 'Using Ohio as a starting point, I cross referenced the name Ulmer with the national census taken in 2010 and found there were only a hundred and fifty people registered with that last name in the entire state. It seemed like a lot, but I got lucky and found his sister on the third try.'

This was amazing detective work. For a gym instructor, she could make one heck of an investigator. She was pulling all of us into the story, the room silent as we waited for her to deliver the big reveal.

'What do you think the website was for?' she asked us and got a sea of blank faces in return. With a big beaming grin, she said, 'A dog sharing service.' She dropped it like a bomb on the room. There was the connection, but she wasn't finished yet. 'Chester's sister, Mary-Louise had some choice words to say about Howard Berkowitz. You told me he had an affair a bunch of years ago and wondered how the stalker knew about it. Guess whose sister he had the affair with.'

Schneider, Baker, and Bhukari all swore at the same time. I had to agree with their sentiment. Howard had been lying through his teeth the whole time. He said the woman was married with her own kids now and had no interest in him. That clearly wasn't true.

Barbie waited for the cussing to subside and then continued. 'According to Mary-Louise, Howard stole the whole idea for his dog website from Chester. Chester lived in the same area and had set up his business. Howard needed someone to look after his wife's dog, but when he discovered what Chester was doing, he bought the company and turned it into a billion dollars in just a few years. He never gave Chester Ulmer any credit for coming up with it.'

I frowned as I thought about what she had just said. 'But Chester sold the idea to Howard. He gave it up. That Howard then went on to make a fortune with it didn't defraud or steal from Chester.'

Barbie shrugged. 'That's not how Chester saw it. Mary-Louise said he went back to Howard to ask for more money and was seized upon by Howard's lawyers. Chester had signed a non-disclosure agreement that stopped him from ever revealing it was his idea.'

Lieutenant Bhukari asked, 'How much did Chester sell his firm for?'

Barbie made an oops face. 'A thousand dollars.'

The sum was immaterial, of course. No one had forced Chester to sell his idea, and had he not sold it, there was nothing to suggest that he could have ever turned what he had into anything worth having. Chester had been affronted by the money Howard made, but his hatred was fuelled by regret that he hadn't done what Howard proved could be. Howard hadn't done anything to Chester, but he had chosen to lie about knowing who Chester was. It wasn't the only lie though: Shandy had lied about having a dog unless the details of the story, as Barbie told it, were inaccurate and that was curious.

Pippin threw his arms in the air. 'Where does this leave us?' We all looked his way. 'Chester Ulmer sent hate messages and came on board the ship with the express purpose of killing Howard and Shandy Berkowitz. Someone fired two shots at the party after rigging the lights to go out, and the target was Mrs Berkowitz and/or her sister; both were hit, one fatally. Mr Berkowitz buys an expensive, undetectable gun and smuggles it on board and the calibre of bullet matches that used to kill Grace Snoke, and both Dr Kim and Nurse Halloran. The evidence suggests Mr Berkowitz is the killer, yet all the motive suggests it was Chester

Ulmer. What I cannot fathom, is why Dr Kim and Nurse Halloran were killed in the first place and who took a shot at Mrs Berkowitz in the mall.'

He did a great job of summing up the confusion we all felt. Instead of working the case out, we were less sure of the solution than we were in the aftermath of the first shooting.

'Did I not help?' asked Barbie, sounding worried that she'd tried to put a fire out by throwing a handy liquid onto it only to discover it was gasoline.

My stomach rumbled, which was cue enough that a break was in order. I put my arm around Barbie's shoulders and twitched my head at Sam. 'I think we should get some lunch, don't you?'

Sam's eyes lit up. 'Ooh, yeah. I am getting hungry, Mrs Fisher.'

I wheeled Barbie around toward the door, calling over my shoulder. 'We'll be back in a little while. I need some space to sort out my head.'

From behind us as we filed from the master bedroom, I heard a chorus of acknowledgements from the security team. Lunch was necessary, but I grabbed for my phone because I had a couple of messages to send, and a phone call to make.

A Tragic Lunch

I sent Sam back to his mother. She had last seen him looking upset about the death of the girl he met. I could tell it was affecting him by how quiet he'd been all morning and I didn't want him around for what I knew was going to happen at lunch. I didn't want Barbie there either, but I knew she had to be. I could have warned her, but ... well, I wanted her reaction to be natural.

My phone call was to my good friend Verity to see what she was up to today. She gave no indication that she was going ashore, and I wondered if, like a lot of people, she had already seen enough of Iceland and wanted to move on.

The ship wasn't going anywhere until it was signed off as seaworthy though, according to Alistair, most of the repairs were cosmetic. Bouncing off a few icebergs hadn't pierced the hull, but it had put a few ugly dents and scars in it and that was not what Purple Star Cruise Lines wanted people to see. Also, the damage Robert Schooner did when he infiltrated the ship's engineering systems all had to be checked over and each system recommissioned to show it wasn't going to suddenly stop working on our way to the next destination or the one after that.

I was right about Verity, she was only too pleased to have an excuse to get out of her cabin and have some company other than her husband, though she didn't actually say that. She promised to join us as soon as she could get from her cabin to our current location. I had guessed correctly that Shandy would gravitate toward the nearest place to get a drink, so we were all in the top deck restaurant and bar at the front of the ship. The fantastic views through high windows along both sides gave the impression of flying above the waves when the ship was in motion. It was a dull, grey day outside today, with light snow sprinkling down to cover every surface with a flawless blueish white blanket.

Shandy wasn't exactly smashed when we spotted her, but she appeared to have imbibed several large cocktails and was on a one-way trip to sloshedville if she didn't slow down. I left Agent Garrett at the bar, asking him to keep watch from there while the ladies had lunch. On the face of it, asking him to eat his lunch elsewhere seemed quite rude, but I knew he was relieved to be able to relax and not listen to women jabbering.

I took a table that gave me an oblique view of Shandy. She was using her phone, though whether she was sending messages or booking flights, I couldn't tell.

A waiter approached with menus, Barbie appearing behind him as she needed to return to her room to change – there is a dress code in the upper deck restaurant, and it does not allow for sportswear. She accepted a menu and took her seat, the waiter deftly manoeuvring it under her bottom as she sat.

I took an extra menu for Verity even though I knew we were not going to get to eat and waited for our other guest to arrive.

'What's Mrs Berkowitz doing?' Barbie asked.

Without looking her way, for it would have been obvious we were spying on her, I said, 'I've only been here a couple of minutes, but she doesn't appear to be doing anything.'

'I wonder how much she knew,' Barbie's eyebrows pinched together. 'She knew they had a stalker, right?'

I nodded, but at the back of my skull a little itch started up again.

Barbie kept on talking, doing her best not to look Shandy's way, but constantly cutting her eyes across the room. 'She must have known where

Howard got the idea for his web-based enterprise.' I tapped my fingers on the table, feeling nervous. I was never a fan of waiting. 'Patty, are you okay?'

I looked up at Barbie, realising now that I must have been projecting how unsettled I felt. 'Sorry, Barbie. My head is full of conflicting information.'

She chuckled a little. 'I should think it would be. I don't know how you work these things out, Patty, but this one seems more confusing than anything before.' She leaned across the table to get close enough to drop her voice. 'Come on, Patty, you must have an inkling. Was it Chester or Howard who pulled the trigger?'

The itch started again, but I got no time to explore why because Verity arrived. A steward was escorting her to join our table. She gave a little wave when I looked her way and was already talking before she joined us. 'Did you know there was another death on board last night?' she asked.

Barbie's eyes widened. 'No. Another one? You don't mean Chester Ulmer, do you?' she asked in response, perhaps wondering if Verity meant another passenger had died and was just confused or ill-informed about where the death had taken place.

Verity let the steward arrange her chair and settled into it before placing her handbag on the deck. 'Chester Ulmer? Isn't that the crazy stalker who shot that poor woman at the anniversary party? No, I heard about him. Didn't he get shot at the airport?'

'That's right,' I replied. 'You're talking about the girl who fell down the stairs.'

Verity nodded in an encouraging way. 'That's right. It's such a terrible tragedy. So many deaths from the same family in one trip. Who would believe it?'

I blinked a few times, not sure what I had just heard. 'The same family?' I repeated her words, seeking clarity.

Verity's eyebrows made a bid for the top of her forehead in a show of surprise. 'Well, Patricia Fisher, and I thought you knew everything that went on around here. The poor girl who fell down the stairs and broke her neck was another of the Berkowitz bunch. She was at the party with us.'

My bottom jaw fell open.

'Are you ready to order ladies?' asked the waiter, appearing by my side though I had not seen him approach. When no one responded, he asked, 'Some drinks perhaps or nibbles while you peruse the menu?'

The shock of Verity's revelations was still rolling over me, but I couldn't respond to her or answer the waiter because I could see Alistair approaching. He had his cap under his arm and Dr Davis was walking just a step behind him. Both wore grim expressions and I steeled myself for what I knew was about to come.

The waiter saw that I wasn't paying him any attention and tracked my eyes to see his captain approaching. Alistair was making a beeline for us and when I next glanced his way, the waiter was nowhere to be seen.

I gulped and felt it hurt my throat. My mouth had gone dry in the two seconds since I saw the captain of the ship approaching. Like the waiter, Barbie saw my thousand-yard stare and followed it to see Alistair nearing our table. She began to smile, but when she saw the utter lack of mirth on his features, her facial muscles let go so that worry could set in.

Stopping at my table, Alistair looked down at me. 'Mrs Fisher … Patricia, I regret to inform you that I have grave news.'

Barbie's hands flew to her mouth with a gasp of horror for what the captain might be about to say next.

'I wish there were another way to break this awful news to you. Thirty minutes ago, Jermaine Clarke suffered a blood clot that made its way to his heart. Dr Davis and his team did everything they could …' I knew Alistair was still talking but I wasn't able to hear his words over the crashing sound of my pulse ringing in my ears and the wailing that Barbie was making before he finished saying the words.

Jermaine had died.

Rope a Dope

Verity was sitting opposite me and next to Barbie with a look of horror etched onto her face. She'd seen Jermaine moving about in my suite and probably spoken to him once or twice, so she knew who he was, but she wasn't emotionally affected by his sudden and unexpected death.

She was making small noises of mutually felt sorrow, the way one does when in the company of awful news, but she didn't know where to look or what to do. Barbie was inconsolable, tears streaming down her face and I needed to get her out of the restaurant and back to the suite as soon as possible.

Feeling like my heart had been ripped out, I got slowly onto unsteady feet and let Alistair take my arm. I held onto him for support and motioned for Barbie to come with me.

She looked up at me with an expression that said everything I felt. Agent Garrett arrived beside me, confusion on his face as he was unaware of the latest tragedy to befall our group. There was still so much to do. Still so many questions to ask about the terrible murders of the last three days, but that would all have to wait now because the news of Jermaine's death took precedence.

To Agent Garrett, I said, 'Help Barbie.' Then I looked down at Verity, who hadn't risen from her seat and couldn't work out what she was supposed to be doing with herself. 'I'm sorry, Verity. I will have to postpone our lunch. Perhaps we can try again in a few days' time.'

She nodded silently, and with half of the people in the restaurant watching, I let Alistair escort me from the room and back to my suite. All the while, my feet moved on autopilot and my brain continued to whirr away at high speed. I wasn't thinking about Jermaine though, I knew there was no need.

Please don't think me callous or uncaring. Like Alistair and Dr Davis, who were in on it because I couldn't do it all by myself, I knew my wonderful butler wasn't really dead at all. Barbie might hate me for making her think that he was, but I needed to be sure that the audience we had would buy the lie. For that, I needed Barbie to be convinced and act accordingly, not know the truth in advance and act convincingly. The two things are not the same.

At my suite, I squeezed Alistair's hand and pulled him into a hug. 'How soon will you repatriate him?' I asked, maintaining the pretence in case anyone was listening.

Alistair replied, 'Tomorrow, before we sail. I will need to send someone to pack his personal belongings.'

I exhaled slowly through my nose, letting myself deflate and with it my shoulders dropped, and I shrank an inch. 'I don't think it has really hit me yet,' I murmured.

'Give yourself a few days, Patricia,' Alistair begged.

Forcing myself to snap out of it, I shook my head to clear it and used both hands to wipe away my tears. Barbie was still sobbing, and to shock her I said. 'No. There is a still a case to crack.' Something Verity said came to mind. 'Dunkirk spirit: that's what this situation requires. Jermaine would tell me to stiffen my upper lip and wade unwavering into the mire if that was what it took. Barbie and I will see to his personal effects. Send someone along later to collect them, please.'

Barbie had a look of utter disbelief on her face: she couldn't believe I thought it was okay to continue with my investigation at a time like this, and if Jermaine were truly dead, I wouldn't. This was all part of the ruse though. I was still the small furry creature being cornered by the cobra, but where before I had thought of myself as the mongoose in the analogy, now I preferred to picture myself as a creature the snake had never seen before. The cobra felt confident because it had slain all who ever came before it. It had a legion of lesser snakes waiting to do its bidding and it knew it was the deadliest creature in the land. What it didn't see was the trapdoor the little furry creature had just walked it over, or the pit of spikes it would fall into below.

I said none of these things. Instead, I came up onto my toes to kiss Alistair's cheek then swiped my keycard over the door panel and went inside. Agent Garrett was doing a good job of steering Barbie, but I grabbed her unresisting hand and pulled her along behind me like a kite flapping in the breeze.

'Patty, I want to lie down,' she protested. 'And I want gin. I want all the gin.'

Anna and Georgie had greeted us at the door as was their habit, but they fell silent when nobody paid them any attention. Perhaps they were able to pick up on emotions, or perhaps it was something even baser than that, but where normally they would bark and get excited, this time they fell into step behind us and followed where we went. Which was directly across the suite, through the kitchen and to the door which led into Jermaine's adjoining cabin.

Turning my body slightly. I sought out Agent Garrett's eyes. He was halfway across the suite and looking confused about what he ought to do next. 'We're going to deal with Jermaine's personal effects now, Wayne. Perhaps you could put the kettle on. I think a nice cup of tea will help everyone.'

He raised his eyebrows in surprise – at my attitude mostly I thought, but he said, 'Right you are, Mrs Fisher.'

'I can't do this now, Patty,' Barbie protested, and she was beginning to become agitated. I could feel her muscles beginning to bunch as she fought against me. She was significantly stronger than me, so it was only by catching her by surprise that I heaved her the rest of the way to the door and shoved her inside.

I got an angry, 'Patty!' before she saw what I needed her to see and she fainted.

'Everything all right?' called Agent Garrett when my limber blonde friend bounced off a chest of drawers on her way to the carpet.

I poked my head back out of the door to find him peering his head around to get a look at what the noise was. I blocked his view quickly.

'It's a bit of a mess, that's all. Jermaine might have kept the suite clean, but Barbie just tripped on a pile of dirty laundry.' I glanced back inside to check on Barbie and found Jermaine frowning at me. He didn't like the suggestion that he was anything other than meticulously neat. I offered him a shrug. 'This shouldn't take us long,' I called to Wayne as I closed the door and carefully turned the lock so it made no noise as it slid home.

With a finger to my lips to stop Jermaine from attempting to speak, I moved in close and gave him a tender hug. I had missed him desperately and his injury – the fact that he got shot – hurt me so terribly that it was akin to getting shot myself. I held him like that, with his right arm wrapped around my back since his left was in a sling, until we heard Barbie begin to stir.

I broke the hug to go to her; I needed to explain several things, but before I could get there, her eyes opened, and she screamed.

I clamped a hand over her mouth which shut her up, but she was hyperventilating and if her eyes had gone any wider the eyeballs might have just fallen out onto the deck.

The door handle started to turn, accompanied by Agent Garrett shouting, 'Everything all right in there?'

'Um,' I pulled a flustered face as I tried to concoct a reason why Barbie had just screamed like she'd seen a ghost. 'Um, we just found Jermaine's porn collection,' I tried. It was Jermaine's turn to show me wide eyes, but he augmented the gesture by throwing his right hand in the air in despair. I think, had he had something to hand which he would throw, he might have bounced it off my head.

'And that made Barbie scream?' asked Agent Garrett sceptically.

'It's some scary stuff,' Barbie replied, pulling herself together and getting in on the lie.

He rattled the door handle again. 'I think you should let me in. Why is the door locked anyway?'

'We need some alone time, Agent Garrett. Make the tea, please. We'll rejoin you soon. Jermaine was our dearest friend.'

I could hear him muttering on the other side of the door, but he moved away, and I heard the kettle begin to get excited a few moments later.

Barbie, accusing eyes narrowed at me, pushed herself upright. 'Patricia Rose Fisher, I cannot believe you let me think he was dead,' she hissed at me angrily. 'I'd better be about to hear that this was absolutely necessary or so help me there will be trouble.'

'I swear I couldn't think of another way to do what needed to be done,' I whispered my reply.

Her eyes remained narrowed when she swung them to pierce Jermaine with the same harsh glare. 'And as for you, Jermaine Clarke. Don't you ever be dead again. Do you hear me? My poor heart feels like it was put through a meat grinder.' She glanced between the two of us, making sure we were both paying attention. 'Now, you horrible pair of tricksters, what are you up to and what do we do next?'

'I can't tell you that just yet,' Barbie's face turned bright scarlet and she looked about ready to explode until I said, 'But I promise to tell you everything soon. First, I have to get out of here and check on something. The case with the Berkowitzs, their stalker, the triple murder, and all the questions about the state of security on the Aurelia needs to be resolved and I think I've just been handed a fat clue.'

Barbie made a gesture like she wanted to throttle me but asked, 'What do you need us to do?'

Gemima

Finding the name of Sam's poor dead girlfriend was easy enough, I just asked Lieutenant Baker. He wanted to know why I asked.

'Because she's another member of the Berkowitz party,' I explained as patiently as I could. I felt a little like adding the word 'dummy' to the end of my sentence though, of course, decorum would not allow it. Why had no one thought to question the connection? There were accidents on board the Aurelia just like there were everywhere else. No matter what precautions are taken, sooner or later someone will find a way to hurt themselves, and stairs are a great place for accidents to happen.

But was Gemima's fall an accident?

I needed to find out.

Lieutenant Baker agreed to meet me so we could visit her parents together. Had they been from New Zealand, I might have questioned the connection myself a little sooner. On the face of it, there was no reason to suspect anything untoward had occurred – it could be nothing but a tragic accident. I wasn't buying it though. There were altogether too many unresolved elements of this mystery and I needed to start sewing them up.

According to Lieutenant Baker, who was reading the information from his handy PDA, Frank and Lekki Smith were from Ohio, where the rest of Howard's family originated. They boarded the ship in Canada, most likely paid for by their billionaire relative, and were along for the anniversary party because Howard and Shandy had chosen to celebrate it with all the people they held dear.

The PDA didn't tell us what their connection to Howard was; I was guessing a distant relationship somewhere, and I was going to find out soon enough. They had another child, a seventeen-year-old girl who was also travelling with them. Gemima had been twenty-five and just a few weeks shy of her next birthday.

Lieutenant Baker knocked on the door with his knuckles, the sound loud in the quiet passageway. They were in one of the staterooms, one down from a suite, on deck eighteen.

It was Gemima's father, Frank, who answered the door. He looked sleep deprived and exhausted. Huge bags hung under his eyes and he was several days past needing a shave. His hair looked like he hadn't bothered to comb it, but what stuck with me most was the haunted look that came from having no emotions left inside his body.

He just looked spent.

'Can I help you?' he asked, his morose voice matching his face.

I let Lieutenant Baker, the man in the ship's uniform speak first. 'Sir, I am Lieutenant Baker. I'm with the Aurelia's security team. The lady beside me is Mrs Patricia Fisher. As part of Purple Star Cruise Lines investigation into the shooting two nights ago at the Berkowitz anniversary party, it is necessary to ask you just a couple of questions.' Frank Smith looked ready to shut the door in our faces, but Baker kept up the pace, never giving him the option to say no. 'I am certain this is not a good time for you, but it is imperative we speak with you and your wife, if she is available, before you depart the ship. I understand you plan to leave in the morning.'

When Lieutenant Baker lapsed into silence, Mr Smith still looked like he wanted to slam the door in our faces. I had never lost a child so could only imagine what he was feeling. It had to be terrible, but if he wanted to tell us to go away, his wife didn't give him the chance. A face appeared behind him through the gap in the doorway.

'Who is it, Frank?' she asked. 'Why have you left them outside in the passageway?'

Doing nothing to conceal his annoyed and frustrated expression, he let go of the door and stepped aside. Walking away into the cabin he grumbled, 'They want to ask questions. You answer them.'

The master bedroom door closed shut a degree louder than was necessary even if it didn't quite register as a slam.

Lekki Smith did not look much different from her husband in that she looked emotionally drained and sleep deprived. In contrast to Frank, she stepped back and out of the doorway, inviting us in first with her body language and then with words. 'Please,' she beckoned. 'Don't think poorly of Frank. He hasn't slept since it happened, and he blames himself.'

'Why is that?' I asked, wondering what reason she might give.

I got a sad look in response. 'A father's prerogative. Anything bad that happens is something that the father ought to have been able to prevent in his opinion. I've seen it in other fathers too. Especially those with daughters. They want to protect them from the world. Sometimes that just isn't possible.'

Lekki looked and sounded like she wanted to cry, but as if all this month's supply of tears had already been depleted, none came.

She was in enough pain without me making her relive it again, but that was what I had come here to do. I thought I had most of this worked out now - there was an itch at the back of my skull to tell me I was on the right path - I hadn't found the evidence that would prove I was right. There were parts though, parts that were intertwined within this mystery that had made it seem so confusing. The confusion came because we were looking at more than one thing but hadn't realised it.

Like trying to do a jigsaw but after hours of trying to work out why the parts don't match up, you discover someone had taken two jigsaws and mixed them up in the same box. Only we didn't have two in the same box, we had three. And none of them matched the picture on the outside of the box they came in.

'Mrs Smith,' I started.

She raised a hand. 'It's Lekki, please.'

I started again. 'Lekki, can I please ask how you are related to the family?' I threw in an easy question to get her talking.

She gave us a half smile. 'I'm Howard's little sister,'

I hadn't expected that, and it felt like I was doing badly in the detective stakes even though I knew the investigation had been advancing at a lightning pace. Logging it away, I got the real question. 'Can you tell me what happened to Gemima, please?'

Her mouth twitched a couple of times and she stared at her fingernails. I thought for a moment she was going to say no, but instead she said. 'I think I need a stiff gin before I go through that again. Will you join me?'

It was unexpected, but not unwelcome and a minute later, I was holding a cold glass of swirling pink liquid. Lekki went for flavoured gins and this one was raspberry. It wasn't what I would usually drink but it was far from unpleasant. Lieutenant Baker, on duty, politely declined the alcoholic beverage and nothing else was offered instead.

When she settled back into her chair, Lekki tucked her feet under herself and sipped at her drink. She didn't make eye contact with either Baker or me, but she did start talking. 'Gemima was a sweet girl, the kind who is always hoping to be of help. I sometimes thought of her as a burden because I knew I would never be free of her, but at the same time, I was blessed because I had a child who would always, always need her mummy. Now I have nothing but guilt for ever wanting to have some time away from her.' She took another sip and let the glass find its way back to her lap where she cradled it with both hands. 'That's not what you wanted to hear though, is it? She tripped and fell so far as we know. She broke her neck and had bruises and cuts but none that would suggest anything else might have happened to her. Who would want to hurt her, anyway?'

I tried a different approach. 'What did she talk about in the last couple of days? Did she have many questions about what happened at the party?'

Lekki looked up finally, meeting my eyes with a gaze that bored into them. 'Why do you ask that?' My question had triggered something. I was here on nothing more than a hunch, but I could tell by her eyes that there was something she concealed that she wanted to reveal.

I made no attempt to fill the void left by her question. I wanted her to do the talking not me. Gemima's mum looked at me for a few seconds as if trying to gauge what kind of person I was before the pressure of the silence in the room overcame her and she began to answer. 'I'm not one for gossip, Mrs Fisher. Nowhere in the bible does it suggest we should talk about the people around us. If I have a question about something, I go up to that person and ask it.'

She had made a statement that failed to reveal anything, and it was clear to me that she was building up to telling me something she was uncomfortable about saying behind the backs of the people it involved.

When I prodded her along, I did so gently. 'What you tell us could be the clue that reveals the identity of Grace's murderer, Lekki. Please share with us whatever it is that you know.'

She bit her bottom lip and looked at her gin. It was half-gone already. 'I don't *know* anything,' she replied before looking up to meet my eyes again. Accepting that she was going to spill the beans, she let her shoulders fall and spat it out. 'Gemima said she saw Uncle Howard kissing Grace.' That wasn't what I was expecting her to say at all. 'I told her she was mistaken or figured she must have misinterpreted what she saw. This was days ago, almost a week before the party and she wouldn't shut up about it. She kept watching the television for people on there to kiss and would then say, "It was like that, mummy". I would look up to find two people embraced in a passionate pose. I dismissed it out of hand. I certainly wasn't going to talk to Howard or Shandy, or even Grace, for that matter. Gemima got upset because I didn't believe her, and it escalated when she told me she was going to ask Uncle Howard about it. It turned into a big fight,' Lekki admitted quietly and a small sob escaped when she said, 'We never got to make up properly afterwards.'

'Did she speak with Howard?' I begged to know. I was leaning forward in my chair, desperate to hear more and wondering what I might have now uncovered. An affair with his sister-in-law?

Lekki shook her head, unable to speak for a moment, and we had to wait half a minute until she managed to blurt out. 'I forbade her to.' There was another wait while she gathered herself. She downed the rest of her gin and I sipped at mine, waiting patiently - because I had no choice, not because I was feeling patient. 'This was right before the party. She was standing right next to Shandy and Grace when the shots were fired. I had just that moment spotted her and wondered if she was being devious and asking Grace or Shandy about what she believed she had seen instead of asking Howard. She could be clever like that; find a loophole in what my instructions. I asked about it afterwards and she swore she didn't, but she was really quiet and thoughtful the whole next day. I asked her why and she said she saw something she didn't understand.' Another tear slipped out and Lekki had to fight against her voice cracking when she said, 'She was still mad at me and wouldn't tell me what it was. She kept saying it didn't matter because I wouldn't believe her anyway.'

Frowning deeply in my frustration, I could sense that I was just away from hearing the clue I needed to stitch the case together, but the only lips that could share that clue had been silenced forever. And that was when it hit me.

'Where are we going, Mrs Fisher?' begged Lieutenant Baker as I all but ran to the nearest elevator.

'Why was Dr Kim killed?' I asked instead of giving him an answer. My question demanded he provide an answer though I knew he had none.

He stuttered a little before trying a guess. 'Because he knew something the killer couldn't risk him revealing?' His voice betrayed how little confidence he placed in his answer, but I thought he was on the money.

'It has to be something like that. He saw something or he heard something. Whatever it was, the killer didn't kill him at the time, but thought it dangerous enough that they needed to go back and ensure his silence later.'

'What about Nurse Halloran?'

I pursed my lips because I didn't like my answer. 'Wrong place, wrong time. Maybe. I guess I don't know. It could be that she was party to the same dangerous piece of information.'

'Why not kill them at the time?' Lieutenant Baker and I were now inside an elevator car and travelling downward. 'We're on our way to sickbay, aren't we?' he sought to confirm.

I nodded, still running things through my head. 'I don't think it was possible to kill them at the time, not without everyone knowing who had done it. The killer had to wait for the right moment to strike. Even though they ought to have been protected by the medical in confidence rule, I believe Dr Kim wanted to tell me, or was going to arrange for me to find out. We'll never know for certain, but when the ballistics report is returned, it will show that Dr Kim and Nurse Halloran were killed with the same weapon that was used on Grace Snoke and Shandy Berkowitz.'

'But that leads us right back to Howard Berkowitz as the killer and we already have him pegged for it with what is starting to feel like overwhelming evidence.'

In the confines of the elevator, I faced Lieutenant Baker and looked into his eyes. 'Howard Berkowitz didn't do it.'

Baker's eyes widened in surprise just as the car pinged and the doors swished open. 'Then who did?'

I was already gone, striding down the passageway to get to sickbay where I expected to find Dr Davis.

Baker got left behind when my last statement rooted his feet to the floor and he almost got caught when the elevator doors closed again. Running to catch up, he asked again, 'Mrs Fisher, who did it if it wasn't Chester Ulmer or Howard Berkowitz.' Then a scary thought occurred to him. 'Who shot your butler? Was it one of them?'

I put a finger to my lips to still his chatter and pushed the door to sickbay open. That I was so familiar with the layout and design of the facility ought to speak volumes about my time on board the Aurelia. Beyond the double doors, wide enough to make entry with a hospital bed on wheels easy, lay a reception area where patients arriving could be triaged and dealt with accordingly. This was the big medical facility on the ship; there were smaller ones on most decks set up to deal with cuts and falls and minor burns. Most of the time it was sunburn and too much alcohol that kept the medical staff busy, but because they might be at sea for days at a time, the sickbay was equipped to deal with broken bones, dislocated joints, heart attacks and minor surgeries. It also had a morgue which got more use that it ought to.

Dr Davis looked up as I came in, surprise showing on his face that he had visitors and that we were not patients seeking care. 'Mrs Fisher, Lieutenant Baker, to what do I owe the pleasure?' he asked.

Baker dipped his head, but he didn't answer because he still had no idea why we were here. I was the one who replied, 'Hello, Dr Davis. All alone?'

'My nurse popped to the restrooms,' he explained.

That made things easier and I got straight to the point. 'I need to see the file on Mrs Berkowitz, particularly the report Dr Kim would have filed on the wound to her neck.'

Dr Davis looked at me deadpan for a moment, waiting for the punchline I thought. When none came, he said, 'Mrs Fisher, that information is medical in confidence. I would be in serious breach of my ethical duties if I were to show it to you. Or allow you to see it,' he added quickly at the end to close one potential loophole.

However, I had no time, and too little interest to go looking for loopholes. Switching to informal, I came closer to him, the doctor rising from his chair as I closed the gap between us until I was standing less than two feet away and craning my neck to look up at his face. 'David, someone killed your friend. I should like to know who it was and by showing me a report and a few pictures, we might catch that person.'

His eyebrows came together as his forehead pinched inwards. 'I thought you already identified the killer?' he glanced at Lieutenant Baker and back at me. 'Didn't Howard Berkowitz murder Dr Kim and Nurse Halloran?'

I shook my head slowly back and forth. 'It was someone else and you are holding the evidence I need to prove it.' Okay, I was overstating the case, but I still needed to see the pictures and read the report to know for sure.

His head was already shaking before I finished speaking. 'It doesn't matter, Mrs Fisher. I cannot breach the confidentiality rule.'

I'd hoped I wouldn't have to do this, but he was leaving me no choice. 'But you would lie openly about the condition of a patient,' I pointed out.

Dr Davis's head snapped around so fast it almost came off his shoulders. 'That's different,' he argued angrily.

'How so?' I raised an eyebrow to encourage him to answer. 'You falsified the death certificate and lied on Jermaine Clarke's paperwork. Or do you think he is actually dead?'

'Wait, what?' Lieutenant Baker was getting confused. 'Jermaine isn't dead?'

I cut my eyes his way and made a shushing noise. 'Blabbermouth. The world must believe Jermaine Clarke is dead which is possible thanks to this man,' I smiled at Dr Davis.

The doctor's lips were flapping up and down. 'But this just makes it worse,' he said. 'If the truth about Special Rating Clarke comes out in the wrong way, it could ruin me.'

'I won't be saying anything,' I promised.

But now it was Dr Davis's turn to narrow his eyes at me. 'If I show you the file, you mean.'

I wagged a finger at him. 'I never mentioned anything of the sort.'

Lieutenant Baker leaned down to whisper in the doctor's ear. When he straightened again, Dr Davis began checking his pockets and then stood up. 'I believe there is an urgent need for me to check on the condition of Mrs Jeffries in 11256. She's been having terrible trouble with her pacemaker. Could you mind the place while I am gone, please? Nurse Lansbury should be back soon.'

With no further discussion, he grabbed his medical bag and left the sickbay, the door swinging shut with him already out of sight.

I gave Baker an impressed look. 'What did you say to him?'

'I sweetened the deal.'

His answer made me frown and pause as I tried to decipher what that meant. In pausing, Lieutenant Baker slipped into the Dr's chair before I could. 'Sweetened it how?' I wanted to know.

Baker was already typing on the keyboard but stopped to offer me a guilty look. 'I told him Barbie had been dating a doctor back in England and was single again. I promised to mention him to her.'

'She's not single,' I pointed out. 'She plans to get back to him as soon as I can deal with the Godmother situation.'

Baker shrugged. 'Dr Davis doesn't know that.'

The line of conversation faded quickly as Lieutenant Baker navigated his way into the file system and found the single entry for Mrs Berkowitz. Silence so complete I could hear the clock ticking on the wall twenty yards away came upon us as we stared at the photograph of her wound. We didn't really need a picture though, just the words Dr Kim had written.

'Here, what are you doing?' asked Nurse Lansbury, scaring the life out of me as she came back through the door just a few feet behind us. Her wipe-clean plastic shoes made no sound on the deck when she walked, and both Baker and I were far too engrossed in what we were doing to have heard the door open.

In a panic, Baker stabbed at the mouse key to kill the screen and succeeded in turning it black before she could get far enough into the room to see what we were looking at.

I spun around with a plastered-on smile. 'Nurse Lansbury, how lovely to see you. Dr Davis rushed out to see a patient and asked us to just mind the place until you returned.'

She didn't meet my eyes or return my smile, she scowled at the computer screen dissatisfied with what I was telling her. 'Were you trying to access patient files?' she asked.

Unwilling to lie directly, I was caught with my mouth hanging open and no words to use.

Lieutenant Baker rescued me. 'Security checks. If I can't get into it, which clearly, I cannot, then it is safe enough.' He got to his feet, stuffing his hat back onto his head, and taking my arm to escort me out. 'Come, Mrs Fisher, we have yet more security work to do.'

Glancing back as I went out of the door, Nurse Lansbury, with a stern expression and fists balled on her hips was watching me go with a suspicious face.

Gathering

'Mrs Fisher?' Molly's voice came through the phone to echo loudly in the elevator. 'Is that you? Agent Garrett has been going nuts!'

Ah, yes. Agent Garrett. Once again, I ditched him to set off by myself. I regretted that I needed to do so, choosing to sneak out via the door to Jermaine's adjoining butler's cabin. I could have taken him with me, but I wanted greater freedom to move, plus I was feeling more and more convinced that no one was going to take a shot at me any time soon.

I chose to ignore her comment about my policeman bodyguard. 'Yes, Molly, it is me. I need you to do something for me. Please get the original copy of the typewritten letter the stalker sent to Mrs Berkowitz and meet me at the ballroom on the upper deck.'

'The one where they had the party the other night where everyone got shot?' she tried to confirm, exaggerating the facts as was her trait because only two people were actually shot.

'Yes, Molly. I will be there soon. Please wait for me.'

I got an, 'Okay,' in response.

'Molly, is Barbie there, please? I'd like to ask her something too.' There was a thing that was bothering me, and it was to do with the lights going out. I knew how that had been achieved: the engineering team found a clever little box fitted inside the circuit, but how did the killer know how to do that?'

'Patty?' Barbie's voice appeared on Molly's phone. 'Molly says you need something?'

I explained what I needed her to do and apologised for how time sensitive it was. Then I wished her luck, ended the call and dialled the next person on my list. Standing beside me, Baker was using his radio to summon help, drawing not only on the team of security guards assigned to assist me in this case, but three times that as we tried to bring as many of the party attendees back to the ballroom as we could.

My first call had been to Alistair, who met me outside the elevator when it reached the top deck. I stepped out and stopped right in front of him, coming to rest with our bodies separated by maybe an inch. Lieutenant Baker slipped by with a crisp salute which Alistair returned.

Alone with Alistair, but with the sound of lift music playing behind me, I felt like putting my arms around him and slow dancing. There would be time for that later, I knew, but as I smiled up at him, I could feel changes within myself that were going to have consequences for my future.

'Are you sure?' he asked.

I kept my smile in place even as a paranoid flicker of doubt shot through me. 'As sure as I can be. It all adds up.'

I got a small shake of his head. 'I don't know how you manage to unravel all the threads, Patricia. I truly do not. You still think pretending your butler is dead was necessary?'

'More so than ever.'

He flipped his eyebrows, accepting he had to hope that I knew what I was doing. He crooked his elbow for me to slide my arm into it and began to walk. We were heading for the ballroom, but he was there only to keep the myriad people under control until I was ready. There was setting up to do and he was going to play the host. It was to be like an impromptu gathering; as many of the attendees from the party two nights ago as possible, because somehow, in just under forty-eight hours, I had figured it out.

Molly was waiting outside of the ballroom as was Barbie, doing her best to still look tearful from the sudden and recent 'death' of Jermaine, and behind them, glaring over their heads was Agent Garrett.

He could glare all he wanted; I wasn't about to apologise for leaving the suite without him. He was in a difficult position because he believed he was required to fend off would-be assassins. I no longer thought he was, but because I also believed there would be moles in his organisation, I couldn't tell him my theories. Besides, I had Lieutenant Baker with me the whole time.

The ballroom was filling up, Lieutenant Baker's rally to get help resulting in over two dozen security guards mucking in to find and round up the various guests from their cabins on the ship or wherever else they might have got to. We wouldn't get them all, and that didn't matter so long as we had the key players. The guest of honour, so to speak, would be joining us last and had no idea this was happening yet. That was Alistair's real purpose for who can resist a dashing man in uniform?

I knew I couldn't.

'I found what you asked for, Mrs Fisher,' said Molly holding up the plastic wallet with the type-written message inside it.

I took it from her and held it up to read again, murmuring, 'Thank you, Molly,' while my eyes danced along the lines. I wasn't wrong, but I needed to give credit where it was due. Molly was heading into the ballroom, looking around and wondering what was going on since I was yet to tell her. 'Hold on, Molly,' I called to stop her.

She spun back around to face me, her expression quizzical.

'Alistair have you met, Molly?' I asked him, certain that he hadn't.

'We haven't yet been introduced,' he conceded, extending his hand. 'Captain Alistair Huntley.'

Molly's eyes widened and she stared at it like it was a creature's tentacle about to yank her to a watery grave. Before I needed to say anything, she took it, and gave a little curtsy, much to Alistair's amusement. 'Pleased to meet you,' she stammered, looking terrified.

'Molly doesn't know it yet, but she solved the case,' I told Alistair while watching Molly.

'I did?' she asked having no idea what I was referring to. 'Yes. Molly is rather observant, you see. She spotted things which I had not.'

'Is that so?' asked Alistair, clearly wondering where I was going with this.

Smiling as I lined up the trap door under her willing feet, I asked, 'Did you know that she is thinking of applying to join the Purple Star Cruise Line security team?'

Molly turned bright purple when Alistair looked at her properly for the first time. 'Is she really? Have you given it serious thought?' he asked her.

Now she was pinned. It was either a fanciful fantasy which she would never find the courage to pursue, or she could choose to walk through the door which was now swinging open for her. Not that she couldn't be happy being a housemaid, or in any other role, but she was young, and her attraction to the life of adventure and purpose on board a cruise line was clear for all to see.

Nervously she said, 'I think I would be good at it.'

Alistair approved of her reply. 'Then I shall see to it that I put in a good word on your behalf. I believe there is a new intake of trainees at the Los Angeles company headquarters shortly.'

'Los Angeles,' she murmured as if all her dreams were coming true.

I put a hand on her shoulder and used it to turn her around and steer her into the ballroom. It was show time.

Big summary

It took more than thirty minutes to get everyone set up, but thanks to Alistair, they were entertained while it happened. Stewards passed between the guests with trays of canapes, hastily made fresh, of course, not the ones left over from the aborted anniversary party. Others brought drinks – alcoholic and soft since there were children present. We had about seventy percent of the original guest list. A few had left already, choosing to abandon the rest of the trip in favour of flying home, and yet others were still ashore somewhere. It was of no consequence.

While that went on, I took the typed message and walked back to my suite. I needed to check something. The original message had been folded in two about the centre line, possibly just to give it rigidity for when it was slid under the door. Outside the door to my suite, I placed one knee on the deck to see how easily it would go under.

Walking back to the ballroom a few seconds later, I could tick off another question from the list in my head. By the time I arrived back at the scene of the party, Lieutenants Baker and Bhukari were doing their best to position everyone. They had the chart of the room between them, the printed version of course, though it threatened to tear a few times as they argued about whether one person or another was correctly positioned in relation to another.

The guests were, for the most part, cooperative. The one man who wasn't, the same man who chose to make demands of his wife, Alice, two nights ago when she volunteered answers, was shouted down by his wife before any of the security crew needed to have a word. Suitably silenced, he fumed and demonstrated his childish nature by refusing to eat or drink any of the drinks and nibbles as they went by. His wife ignored him to chat with the guests around her.

Once I got the nod that they were ready, I found Alistair. He was being his naturally charming self, passing through the crowd where he could engage small groups with anecdotes or remarkable facts. When I caught his eye, he detached himself from the people he was with, making the excuse that he was needed elsewhere.

'It's time?' he asked.

I nodded. 'Please.'

'Still think you are right?'

Having seen the type-written note again, I knew I was. The note wasn't enough to secure a conviction. Nor was any of the other evidence I had so I was going to do what I could to lure the guilty person into giving themselves away.

I watched Alistair leave the room, gave him five minutes, by which time I figured he must be on his way back and took a deep breath. My stomach was alive with butterflies as I walked to the stage and stood on the same spot, more or less, that Howard had occupied that night.

'Ladies and gentlemen,' I called to get everyone's attention.

'Why are we here?' shouted Alice's annoying husband, thinking he spoke for everyone in the room.

I swung my attention his way. 'Thank you, sir, that is a good question. I want to thank you all for coming.' I had their attention, everyone in the room looking my way now. It was already dark outside, just as it had been on the night, but the lights were not turned down to create a more intimate party atmosphere tonight, they were set to their maximum which bathed the room in light. 'We are here because the matter of who killed Grace Snoke and wounded Shandy Berkowitz is yet to be resolved.'

'Haven't you heard?' joked Alice's husband. 'Howard pulled the trigger. I thought everyone knew that.' He looked around for support, but none came, which left him feeling smaller and more foolish than I could have managed with a harsh retort.

I drew in a deep breath through my nose to calm myself just as Alistair came back into the room, and the two guards positioned by the doors, swung them slowly closed to seal us all in. 'You have been arranged tonight according to the positions you were in when the shots were fired. This is as close to a recreation of the event as we can achieve at short notice. There are of course two vital people missing from the equation: Grace and Shandy. Here comes Shandy now.'

Alistair had Shandy on his arm, much like he would if he were with me. He led her around the front of the gathered crowd to get to the spot reserved for her. Looking about at everyone in the room, she asked, 'What's going on?'

Lieutenants Schneider and Pippin were on hand to greet her and make sure she was in position back where she had been when she got shot.

Ignoring her question, I continued to explain to everyone else. 'That takes care of Shandy, and for tonight, Grace will be played by one of my colleagues.' Barbie stepped forward and into position next to Shandy. 'There is one other vital person I need to substitute because there was another tragic death last night. Gemima Smith, Howard's niece, fell to her death as I am sure you all know, and for the purposes of this exercise, her position will be taken by another of my colleagues.' I had already briefed Molly about her role, my soon-to-be-former housemaid taking up position a few feet from Barbie. Her parents Lekki and Frank were not here and there were two good reasons for that. The first of which was that I thought it would be too hard for them, and the second ... well, I'll tell you in a minute or so.

'Why is she looking at me?' asked Shandy because Molly was the one person in the room who was not looking at the stage.

'Is that not what Gemima was doing on the night?' I asked. I didn't wait for an answer though, moving swiftly on because I had a lot to get through and didn't want to lose the crowd's attention. 'You have all heard that a gun was found and that it belonged to Howard. How that information got out,' I was fairly sure Shandy leaked it herself much like she told everyone about her stalker, 'is not important. The fact is that even though he owned the weapon and snuck it aboard the ship, he was not the one who brought it to the party.'

'What?' asked Shandy. 'My Howard is innocent? I thought you said he was the one!' Her hands grabbed for either side of her face. 'Oh, God, what have I done?'

I took control of the room again. 'I will ask you to just accept for now that Howard didn't pull the trigger, but we all know that someone did. Two people were shot at the party, and that is an important factor as I will shortly demonstrate. The one person it couldn't have been is Shandy because she was standing opposite the killer and got shot herself.'

I paused for effect and to give myself a second to gather my thoughts before pressing on. 'Some of you might have known before but you all know now that the Berkowitzs had attracted a stalker. A man by the name of Chester Ulmer is the man who invented *Walk my Dog.com*.' A collective gasp went around the room and I had to raise my hands and my voice to regain calm. 'Howard bought the dot com company from Chester legitimately and then went on to make a fortune from it. There was nothing untoward or underhand about Howard's actions that I am aware of, but Chester, seeing the money Howard made, decided he was owed more than the sum agreed when he sold the firm.

For months, Chester Ulmer has been sending Howard and Shandy hate-filled emails, demanding restitution, and when their continued ignorance became too much, he tracked them here, infiltrating Shandy's social media to discover what she was doing and where she would be.'

Shandy put a hand to her chest. 'Really? He knew we were here because of me?'

Once again, I chose to ignore her. 'Chester Ulmer came here to kill Howard and Shandy in a spiteful act of self-driven vengeance. But he didn't kill Grace and he didn't shoot Shandy. Mr and Mrs Berkowitz had no idea their stalker was on board the Aurelia.'

'Yes, they did!' snorted Alice's husband, making a nuisance of himself yet again. 'He hand-delivered them a note that morning. He stuck it under their door.'

This time, I noticed that the imposing form of Lieutenant Schneider was moving through the crowd to position himself a pace behind and just to the left of the annoying man. It shut him up, but I was ready to field his argument anyway.

'No, he didn't, actually. There was a typewritten note, and it was sent by the killer, but not by Chester Ulmer.' I could see I was losing people, the crowd struggling to follow what I was telling them.

It was time to explain. 'The killer messed up. Americans spell a lot of words differently from the British. Colour, Honour, etcetera. Lots of them, but they were all spelled the American way in the emails which Chester wrote. Not so in the typed letter that came under the door. In the typed letter, they were spelt the British way, and do you know of another nation who uses the British spelling for most words?'

'New Zealand!' shouted a man in the crowd. 'We spell things correctly.'

I ignored the jibe about Americans choosing to drop letters where they fancy for in truth it is the British who chose to add them after the settlers from Britain had already taken the language across to America with them. 'The fact is that the typed message had the same flavour and feel to the threats contained therein, but it wasn't crafted by the same person. Why was it printed and pushed under the door and not emailed as before? If Chester Ulmer wants to kill them, the last thing he should do is tip them off that he is here and limit his chances of getting close to them.' I paused to gather my thoughts again. 'You might wish to argue that he wasn't in a sane frame of mind, and you might be right, but the paper used for the note is the high-grade paper the cruise line ships in from a printers on Oxford Street in London. It is reserved only for the suites on the top two decks.' I let that sink in for a second. 'Chester could not have easily got his hands on it.' I looked around the room making eye contact with as many of the guests as possible. 'By a process of elimination, the killer is a person from New Zealand who is staying in a suite. The killer also had to be someone close to the Berkowitzs as he or she knew enough about the threatening emails to be able to recreate one, but they didn't have the skills to send it via the internet without leaving a trail and had to print it.'

'In the aftermath of the shooting, when poor Shandy was cradling her sister and holding the wound to her neck to staunch the bleeding, someone saw something that got them killed. That someone was Gemima Pauline Smith. I never got the chance to meet Gemima, but I am told she was a delightful girl. Due to her Downs Syndrome, she couldn't see the danger in revealing what she knew and in so doing, she spoke to the wrong person.'

On cue, Molly raised her right hand to identify herself. 'What did you see, Gemima.'

Speaking boldly, Molly, playing the role of Gemima, said for all to hear, 'I saw Aunt Shandy putting a gun back into her handbag.'

This time, the collective gasp was augmented by shrieks of surprise and comments of denial. Shandy was staring right at me and grinning. 'Hold on. Didn't you say just a couple of minutes ago that it couldn't have been me because I was facing the killer. How is it that you think I shot my own sister and then myself? Why would I even want to?'

'Because Grace was sleeping with Howard,' I stated flatly. I was guessing now, making a leap because it linked all the other clues together and made sense.

Shandy's smile faltered for a heartbeat, and in that moment, I knew I was right. 'You kept your hand on the wound to your neck until they took you from the room, didn't you?'

'It was bleeding heavily,' she chuckled. I was coming down off the stage now and crossing to get into her face. 'I might have bled out if I hadn't plugged the hole.'

'But there was no hole, Shandy, was there?' Now her grin was in serious jeopardy of slipping right off to smash on the deck. 'The bullet nicked your skin and made it bleed, but not so much as the cut you made yourself to ensure there was blood flowing down your neck. You had to hide that from everyone.'

'You're barking mad,' she sneered.

'That wasn't the only thing you needed to hide though, was it? Dr Kim asked you about the powder burn on your neck, didn't he? That's why you had to kill him. You might have always planned to kill him, or you might have decided it was necessary after you heard he was trying to contact me. It's why you gave the guards in your suite the slip. You were wise enough to stop for lunch on the way back from murdering two people, trying to create an alibi of sorts. That's when you tossed the gun over the side isn't it?'

She chuckled again, playing to the crowd as a defence to my accusations and trying to make them sound foolish. 'Create an alibi? Are you referring to when you bumped into me in the mall and the real killer tried to shoot me yet again? Or do you think I was also on the mezzanine firing the gun at the same time I was talking to you?' With a broad smile, which did little to hide the fear I could see in her eyes, she panned around to the crowd.

'It's interesting you should say real killer. Who do you think it is, Shandy?'

'Well, it certainly isn't me,' she snorted.

Keeping my tone level, I said, 'It wasn't your husband, Howard, because he was in your suite at the time which can be confirmed by the guards minding it.'

'Then it was Chester Ulmer, taking another shot at me,' she claimed, sounding confident.

'But he never made it back onto the ship after going to the hospital, Shandy.' Her smile froze again. 'The fact is that the person who shot at you in the mall has not yet been identified. But we do know it was neither of the other suspects.'

I got a proper laugh from her this time. 'All of this postulating only to admit that you don't know who fired the weapon. Excuse me, I think I'll be going now.' Shandy made to move, but I stopped her with my next sentence.

'Why did you kill Gemima? I guessed that she saw you putting a gun in your bag when the lights came back on but maybe she saw you step forward to take the shot, or she may have seen you cut your neck. Which was it, Shandy?'

'This is ridiculous,' she growled getting angry now.

I pursed my lips and stared her down. 'Howard's sister, Lekki, tells a different story. Gemima told her what she saw. Unfortunately, Lekki didn't believe her, which is why Gemima came to you last night, isn't it?'

'You've no proof,' Shandy insisted.

'The guards on your suite were called away after Chester was shot and killed at the airport. The threat from the stalker was eliminated, but not the threat from you. You had ditched the gun by then, and with Chester dead, you could no longer kill with the hope that people would think it was the stalker covering his tracks somehow. That was why you shoved her down the stairs. She wouldn't even have suspected anything was amiss when you invited her to take a walk.'

'You've still no proof,' she hissed.

'Of you killing Gemima? No, that's correct, I don't.' She grinned again, snorting at my incompetence but the room was silent bar for a susurration of murmurs, and it was clear to me that the audience were not on her side. 'You looked nervous at the party; I remember commenting on it. You used it as an opportunity to tell me about your stalker, sowing the seed of the crazed killer into yet another mind. The stalker wasn't causing the nerves though; you had no idea he was genuinely on board. It was the build up to your crime that had you on edge. Would the lights go out as you planned? Fitting an overload device you could control with your phone was a neat touch, by the way. It threw me for a while until I remembered that your father was an electrician.' I watched her face, waiting for the confusion to show. 'Oh, that's right, he was a carpenter, wasn't he? That's what you tell everyone. It's not true though, is it, Shandy? Your father was an electrician and you used to work with him. Isn't that right?'

Shandy refused to answer and I glanced at Barbie, who said, 'You probably haven't thought about your employment record for years, Shandy.' The eyes in the room swung in Barbie's direction. 'It was on LinkedIn together with your qualifications.'

A vein began to throb on the side of Shandy's forehead as tension built and attention swung back to me as I came in for the kill. 'Gemima saw Grace and Howard kissing a week ago and her mother stopped her from saying anything. Had she not done so, maybe none of this would have come to pass. Or maybe Chester Ulmer would have got to kill you before you could kill your sister.' My voice was building to a crescendo now, getting louder with each sentence as I forced my points home. 'You saw an opportunity to use the threats in the emails. You could kill the lights, step forward and shoot your sister at almost point-blank range. Then you fired another shot right next to your neck so everyone would know you were standing next to her. The concept of a stalker had been quietly, yet widely publicised by you so everyone would assume the killer was a crazy person with a grudge. But you hadn't counted on the real stalker tracking you here. You almost got away with murdering four people.' I let my voice soften again. 'You did a good job of pretending you didn't know about Howard's gun. You convinced me, but now you'll have to convince a judge.'

'Why?' she sneered. 'I don't think you can prove any of it.'

I shook my head sadly. 'I don't have to, Shandy. The legal team for the prosecution will do that. Your lawyers, fine ones I'm sure with your money, will try to fight it, but the evidence when they begin to investigate your crimes more fully will soon stack up. Look at how easily your lies came apart in just the two days I have been investigating. You lied about knowing who the stalker was. You lied about having dogs. You lied about knowing where the gun was. Right now, a team is in your suite looking for the dress you were wearing that night. You ensured your right hand was covered in blood to hide the gunshot residue on it, but there will be plenty on the dress.'

I paused and moved around, eyes in the room tracking my movement as I ran a final mental checklist. Content I had it all laid out now, I hit her with the coup de grace. 'Do you know what got you caught, Shandy?' She raised a single eyebrow. 'It wasn't the powder burn or the letter with the wrongly spelt words, it wasn't the lies to get rid of the guards so you could kill Dr Kim and his nurse. It was a single word.'

The room was utterly silent as they waited for me to finish.

With every set of eyes on me, I delivered the death blow. 'Supposeably.'

Supposeably?' Shandy repeated.

I nodded my head sadly. 'It isn't a word, Shandy. I heard you say it at the party. Of course, I felt no need to comment and hadn't thought about it since until I reread the note a short while ago. The word is supposedly. I didn't see it the first time I read the typewritten note, it was only when Molly drew my attention to the incorrectly spelled words that I picked up on it: you used supposeably in the fake message you typed and pretended to find poked under your door. I say pretended because it's not possible to shove a piece of paper under the doors.' Her frozen smile looked ready to crack and fall off. 'You didn't know that did you? The door's locking mechanism sends bolts into the floor and ceiling. I assume that is to protect the valuables of the people inside – the passengers in those suites are often among the richest on the planet. I should have seen it sooner, but I didn't, and for that lack of vision on my part, three more people died.'

Lieutenants Baker and Bhukari had moved in to stand behind Shandy, ready to take her into custody. She looked around the room. 'What? You can't seriously believe any of this? It's all utter nonsense. Who was the shooter in the mezzanine? Huh?'

Lieutenant Bhukari spoke quietly but with unwavering firmness. 'I think, Mrs Berkowitz, that you should come with us now.'

Shandy spun about to shove her away as she stepped nearer, but her arms were caught by Lieutenant Bhukari who was faster and fitter by far than the older woman. A brief tussle ensued as they cuffed her amid a lot of inventive swearing.

Alistair came to stand next to me. 'Patricia, I want to say that what you just did, the way you controlled the room, was nothing short of spectacular.'

It was nice to hear the compliment, but I had felt like wetting myself from the first time I spoke until that exact moment. In response to his kind words, I said, 'I think I'd really rather like a gin now.'

The Godmother's Agent

My alarm went off at two thirty the following morning. It felt like a dirty time to be getting woken up, but it had been my idea. Agent Garrett would be asleep, so though I had a natural inclination to include him, as explained earlier, trusting him meant trusting everyone he might then speak to across multiple agencies and that was too great of a risk to take.

To that end, my team were meeting in the silly hours like a clandestine organisation brought together for a deadly purpose. I tiptoed from the suite with Barbie right behind me. Sensibly, she had head to toe black skin-tight sportswear that made no noise and let her move like a cat burglar. I wasn't that bright, thinking only to throw on my dressing gown over my pyjamas. On my feet were pink house slippers.

There was no one around, save for a few security guards who we looked out for and avoided – it was better to just not be seen by anyone. We took the stairs and made our way down to deck eight where at cabin 34782 we quietly knocked.

A voice on the other side said, 'Password,' at a volume no one standing more than a yard from the door would hear.

Barbie gave me a confused look.

'Open the ruddy door, Mike!' I hissed at him, only to hear him snigger as he undid the lock on the other side.

We were the last to arrive for the first meeting and the people in Mike's cabin were all waiting for me. It was a team I not only wanted to trust but knew I absolutely had to. It was cramped in the small space with so many of us in there, but the four lieutenants: Baker, Schneider, Bhukari, and Pippin were joined by Alistair who believed he had a personal stake in my survival. Next to Alistair was Mike and squeezed in beside him was Jermaine. Sam was grinning at me from a cushion on the deck because there just weren't enough seats to go around and with Barbie at my side that made ten of us. It wasn't enough.

'Hello, everyone. Sorry to disturb your sleep like this.'

Barbie patted my shoulder as she squeezed around me to take up a spot behind Jermaine so she could hold his hand. 'It's okay, Patty. We're all in this together. Just tell me why we had to fake Jermaine's death, please. You promised to tell me and now it's time to spill the beans.'

'The unidentified shooter on the mezzanine,' I told her. 'That's why.'

My assembled friends exchanged glances. All except Mike, who knew where this was going already.

'You've all met Mike, yes?' I asked.

I got a round of yesses and nods, but Barbie asked, 'Yeah, what's with that Patty? What is Mike, a cop from England doing here?'

'He's doing what no one else could. He's helping me catch the Godmother.'

Barbie stared at me. 'I thought we were here to escape the Godmother while the police go after her. Wasn't that the plan?'

I puffed out my cheeks. 'That was the lie we told the police. It was never a plan that was going to work though. They haven't been able to catch her so far and they have no idea who she is. I, at least, know what she wants. She wants me dead and she wants to see me suffer in the process. To do that she will need to place agents close to me. I counted on her organisation having people inside the various law enforcement agencies that are after her. How else would she stay ahead of them? To me, it seemed highly probable that she would discover where I was and send agents after me. To be sure,' I admitted cautiously, 'I left a breadcrumb trail for her to follow.'

'You think there are terrorists on board this ship right now?' asked Alistair, filled with concern.

'Not terrorists per se, although they might blow things up to get what they want. Assassins would be a more accurate term. I think. One of them shot Jermaine.'

It was like laying down a fifth ace in a poker game and it shocked everyone in the room.

Jermaine said, 'You think I was the target?'

He got a slow nod from me in return. 'I'm sure of it. Once I eliminated the possible people connected with the Grace Snoke murder – they all had alibis – I had to start wondering who else would shoot at her, but it was Lieutenant Baker who tipped me off.'

'I did?' he asked, no idea what I was talking about.

'You said it was impossible to miss from that distance,' I reminded him.

He scoured his memory, 'I did say that.'

'And you were right because the shooter didn't miss. They were aiming at Jermaine. There are agents of the Godmother on board and they are here to eliminate me and all those around me, but not in that order.'

'What do you mean?' Barbie asked, dread filling her voice.

I sighed and plunged onward. 'I think they mean to kill all of you first as punishment. The Godmother wants to see me suffer and only then, when I am broken, will she let me die.'

Pippin said, 'Wow. That's some crazy level of hate she has going for you if that's the case.'

Alistair wasted no time on such observations. 'What can we do, Patricia? You always seem to have a plan.'

It was so good of him to lead me nicely to my next point. 'I guess you could say that this is what I hoped for. Mike came on board to watch the people watching me. Anyone who was paying me close attention or trying to be my friend was background checked by Mike because I felt certain he would discover someone wasn't who or what they said they were.'

'And did they? Lieutenant Bhukari wanted to know.

Mike nodded.

'Well who is it, Patty, come on!' squealed Barbie, her impatience overflowing.

I took a second before answering, thinking about how I wanted to present the information because too much too soon would scare them. 'Before I tell you, I want to talk to you about what has to come next. The Godmother runs an organisation called the Alliance of Families. I don't know much about it, but then I don't think anyone really does. Chester Ulmer is not the one who brought an assault rifle on board; that was the Godmother's people. It is likely they have been able to get to members of the Aurelia's crew and bribed or blackmailed, possibly even threatened them into helping them bring weapons on board. Make no mistake, they are very dangerous.'

'If we wound them, it will be like wounding a great white shark: it will turn around in a flash and bite us in half. We might as well have not bothered. To win, we must lure the shark to the surface so slowly that it has no idea it is following our bait. The hook will go into its mouth so carefully, it will not even realise what it was biting until the time is right. It is the most dangerous fish in the water, and it knows it. The only way to beat it, is to let it believe that it has beaten us. That is why Jermaine had to die. Jermaine will remain dead until this is over, because the longer the shark thinks its prey is defenceless, the more powerful the prey's final surprise becomes. At the end, the shark will leap willingly onto the boat and only then, when it is too late, will it understand what has happened.'

Silence settled over the small cabin as everyone took a few moments to absorb what I had just told them. The silence continued until Barbie snapped her fingers. 'I've just worked out who you are talking about.' Everyone, including me, looked at her. 'The agent of the Godmother. The one who has been trying to get close to you. It's Verity.'

'Wait a second,' Jermaine screwed up his face. 'You think Verity Tuppence is an agent of the Godmother?'

I shook my head. 'No, sweetie. Verity Tuppence, is the Godmother.'

The End

Author's Note

Good evening, dear reader,

I suppose, of course, that it may very well not be evening when you read this, but it is evening where I am.

Where am I? I live in the south east of England in a county called Kent. It is referred to as the garden of England because there is so much produce grown here. I only need to drop a seed in my garden, and it springs to life. When I walk my dogs, a pair of miniature dachshunds, I find myself among vineyards and orchards within a few minutes. It officially turned autumn just a couple of days ago and in this part of the world that is a magical time. The air takes on a quality that, even as a wordsmith, I could not hope to describe. It's like woodsmoke mixed with pine and that insanely attractive scent you get when it has just rained after it hasn't rained for ages. I just walk around smelling the air like a crazy person. I hope you have some version of that to enjoy yourself.

This book was something of a pivotal point for the series. Of course, when I wrote the first Patricia Fisher book and started with my idea of ruining her life only to show how much better it could be, I had no idea I would get beyond a trilogy, let alone make it to book seventeen. There is no end in sight, and at this point, I honestly wonder how far I can take it. I have read series that went on far longer than they ought to have, and I do not want that for Patricia. It will have to end eventually, heck, so will I, but I hope to complete her story before I cash my chips in. Anyway, a pivotal point because I had several decisions to make about where the series and Patricia's life in particular were going.

I believe the choices I have made, and will be crafting the story around over the next few books, will please all the readers.

A few months ago, when COVID first hit, I started remarking on what was happening and how it was affecting the community around us. Like most people (I think) I expected the restrictions imposed would last for a while and be annoying but entirely bearable. We are in month seven now and there is no sign that it is going to end any time soon. It is our new reality, and my small children, five months and five years, one boy and one girl, will grow up knowing little else. Hunter, the elder, turns five this Sunday and there will be no party like there has been other years. He is just one of the millions affected in a small way, because there are so many affected in significant ways too terrible to mention. His complaints, while genuine, are too trivial for adults, but the whole world when you can perceive nothing beyond the tiny village you live in.

From the finish of this book, I move to write the next Albert Smith Culinary Caper. After that, I am starting a brand-new series with all new characters, but don't worry, I will be back writing Patricia before you know it. The Godmother, her eighteenth outing, will not be her last, not by a long way; I can perceive the next five or six books already. Over the next few years, her story will continue to develop, so stick around, it's going to be murder.

Take care

Steve Higgs

What's next for Patricia Fisher?

Can an English middle-aged cleaner with a brain for solving mysteries really take down a global organised crime firm? She'd better hope she can because they are not taking her past insults lightly.

The Godmother, head of the Alliance of Families, wants Patricia Fisher dead, but she wanted it so bad, she placed herself on the Aurelia right alongside her to make sure it happened the way she wanted.

That was her mistake for Patricia Fisher knows she attracts trouble and was watching.

As the cat and mouse game develops, the two opposing characters will have to work which one of them is the cat.

Be ready for Patricia's craziest adventure yet!

Pork Pie Pandemonium

Baking. It can get a guy killed.

When a retired detective superintendent chooses to take a culinary tour of the British Isles, he hopes to find tasty treats and delicious bakes …

… what he finds is a clue to a crime in the ingredients for his pork pie.

His dog, Rex Harrison, an ex-police dog fired for having a bad attitude, cannot understand why the humans are struggling to solve the mystery.

He can already smell the answer – it's right before their noses.

He'll pitch in to help his human and the shop owner's teenage daughter as the trio set out to save the shop from closure. Is the rival pork pie shop across the street to blame? Or is there something far more sinister going on?

One thing is for sure, what started out as a bit of fun, is getting deadlier by the hour, and they'd better work out what the dog knows soon or it could be curtains for them all.

More Books by Steve Higgs

Blue Moon Investigations

Paranormal Nonsense

The Phantom of Barker Mill

Amanda Harper Paranormal Detective

The Klowns of Kent

Dead Pirates of Cawsand

In the Doodoo With Voodoo

The Witches of East Malling

Crop Circles, Cows and Crazy Aliens

Whispers in the Rigging

Bloodlust Blonde – a short story

Paws of the Yeti

Under a Blue Moon – A Paranormal Detective Origin Story

Night Work

Lord Hale's Monster

The Herne Bay Howlers

Undead Incorporated

Patricia Fisher Cruise Mysteries

The Missing Sapphire of Zangrabar

The Kidnapped Bride

The Director's Cut

The Couple in Cabin 2124

Doctor Death

Murder on the Dancefloor

Mission for the Maharaja

A Sleuth and her Dachshund in Athens

The Maltese Parrot

No Place Like Home

Patricia Fisher Mystery Adventures

What Sam Knew

Solstice Goat

Recipe for Murder

A Banshee and a Bookshop

Diamonds, Dinner Jackets, and Death

Frozen Vengeance

Mug Shot

The Godmother

Albert Smith Culinary Capers

Pork Pie Pandemonium

Bakewell Tart Bludgeoning

Stilton Slaughter

Bedfordshire Clanger Calamity

Death of a Yorkshire Pudding

Free Books and More

Get sneak peaks, exclusive giveaways, behind the scenes content, and more. Plus, you'll be notified of Fan Pricing events when they occur and get exclusive offers from other authors because all UF writers are automatically friends.

Not only that, but you'll receive an exclusive FREE story staring Otto and Zachary and two free stories from the author's Blue Moon Investigations series.

Yes, please! Sign me up for lots of FREE stuff and bargains!

Want to follow me and keep up with what I am doing?

Facebook

Printed in Great Britain
by Amazon